VISITING COMPOSER

VISITING COMPOSER

ANDREA AVERY

MIAMI UNIVERSITY PRESS

Copyright © 2025 by Andrea Avery
Library of Congress Cataloging-in-Publication Data
Names: Avery, Andrea, 1977– author.
Title: Visiting composer / Andrea Avery.
Description: [Oxford] : Miami University Press, 2025.
Identifiers: LCCN 2024044908 | ISBN 9781881163756 (paperback)
Subjects: LCGFT: Novellas.
Classification: LCC PS3601.V4648 V57 2025 | DDC 813/.6—dc23/eng/20241115
LC record available at https://lccn.loc.gov/2024044908
Designed by Crisis
Printed in Michigan on acid-free, recycled paper
Miami University Press
500 Harris Dr.
Miami University
Oxford, Ohio 45056

FOR BETH AND SARAH AND MONICA AND EMERY

VISITING COMPOSER

THE composer Gloria Clifford, disappeared and presumed dead since 1940, appeared in Enid Bluff's twentieth-century music theory class just as the professor climbed the steps to the stage in front of the dim recital hall and called the class to order by running a hand through his wild gray hair and announcing, "Good morning, today will be in the key of D minor," which no one understood but everyone wrote in their notebooks in case they were asked later, on an exam, to supply the key of Wednesday, October 16, 1996.

Before Gloria's appearance—which turned into forty-eight hours that Enid would treasure, mostly privately, for the rest of her life—Enid had never heard of Gloria Clifford. When Enid spotted the unfamiliar girl sitting a few rows ahead of her and to the left, she could not have identified her, could not have immediately perceived the full strangeness of her appearance (in a 200-level music theory course at a middling state school nearly two thousand miles and half-a-century distant from the last time anyone saw her alive). What was weird at first was that the girl was, like Enid, sitting alone.

From the very beginning of their time as music majors—semester-long courses in eighteenth-century theory with Gouger, then nineteenth with Morello and twentieth with Doyle—the students had sorted themselves into a fixed seating arrangement: music theatre majors and "throats" down front, where the stage lights caught the glitter in their face makeup and the sheen in their tights; bed-headed jazzers along the back row so they could keep one eye on the standing basses and skateboards they left parked along the recital hall's back wall when they ambled in late; performance majors (the serious violists and fl*au*tists and horn players) grouped by instrument, an orchestral habit; pianists together but only grudgingly, leaving an empty seat or two between and beside; and the composers in a studious cluster in dead center.

Where, by rights, Enid should have been sitting. She was officially a sophomore, a third-semester music theory and composition major, for the time being, anyway. But from the very beginning, she'd sat alone. Enid was, as the other composers frequently reminded her (in jest, of course!), the "token girl" of the composing program. Earlier that semester, at a required evening guest lecture about the Methodist hymnist Charles Wesley, a classmate had raised his hand to ask, "I know what thieves are, but what are *harlots* and *publicans*?" and a fellow composer had piped up, "That's easy. We're publicans," he swept his arm to indicate the whole class, "and she's the harlot." Enid's professor had laughed and said to the ancient lecturer visiting from some better school, "I guess that makes us thieves."

Whether it was that the guys rejected Enid on account of her sex or that she rejected them on account of their retrograde jokes, the result was the same: they were the real composers, and Enid was (until the Wednesday that Gloria Clifford appeared, and again on Friday when she departed, and thereafter) a cohort of one.

From behind, Enid marked a long, dark braid spilling over the collar of a white blouse and the back of the girl's seat, grazing the knees of an unbothered tuba player. When the clarinetist to the girl's right scrambled to unfold the hinged writing surface and scribble down Dr. Doyle's D-minor greeting, the girl turned her head slightly and Enid caught a glimpse of full cheeks, a jutting chin, and wire glasses on a long, square-tipped nose. Enid wondered if she was another guest speaker invited by Dr. Doyle, but the girl seemed to be the same age as the rest of the students, a pitch above or below twenty. A wunderkind? A mid-semester transfer student? The girl wasn't writing anything down, just watching, arms crossed in front of her body.

Dr. Doyle shook his head, either at the absurdity of his own greeting or at the sight of a roomful of young people obediently writing it down, and crossed to the corner of the stage. "We're going to start with our listening today, class," he said. He pulled a record from its liner and placed it on the turntable. He leaned on the grand piano that sat in its quilted cloak, wheels locked, and twirled the album in his hands. "This is a very important piece of work." He waved the LP in the air; Enid could tell only that the words on its face were in Italian. "You know the drill by now," Dr. Doyle continued. "I want you to write down everything you hear. All the usual stuff: melody, harmony, rhythm, timbre. Just write down what you're hearing. I won't collect it. Then we'll discuss." He turned back to the turntable and moved the arm. Pens hovered above notebooks.

The music students were accustomed to this. Not only had Dr. Doyle done this low-stakes "open listening" exercise at least once a week since the semester started in August, but their music history professor, Dr. Wallace, gave brutal "drop the needle" exams: he would start an unnamed piece of music anywhere and the students were to write down everything that they knew about it. The tests were stressful, almost entirely because of the scoring policy. If you wrote, "This is in 4/4 time" (and you were right), you got 1 of 1, which went into the gradebook as 100 percent. But if you wrote, "This is in 4/4 time" (correct!) and "The clarinets are repeating the opening motive of the flutes" (wrong, those are oboes), you got 1 of 2, a 50 percent in the gradebook. There was no limit to the number of points available on a test, so the best strategy was to write only what you were certain of. Enid had aced a recent test by writing simply *clarinet* on the page. On a separate sheet, she'd written *D-flat major 1850–1890? folk song maybe Russian maybe Borodin?* and then smuggled her crib sheet out of the test so she could figure out later what she'd been hearing, how good her ear was. On her own.

Dr. Doyle was no Dr. Wallace, but he was tough in his own way. The first day of twentieth-century theory, even before he'd handed out the syllabus or told the class his name, he'd held up a small compression spring, like a tiny Slinky. "Listen, class," he'd said, holding the spring between his thumb and finger in the air in front of him. "Do you hear that?" he asked, bouncing the spring silently in front of him. "Isn't that something?" When no one reacted, he stuffed the spring into the pocket of his khakis, sighed, and started passing out the syllabus.

The students weren't exactly worried about his listening exercise this morning. Or, no more worried than usual. Music majors were always coiled with anxiety; a low drone note of insecurity vibrated in every performance space, practice room, and classroom of the music school. How many times had Enid left one of Wallace's drop-the-needle exams and walked out to the covered patio everyone called the Smoking Section, and no sooner had she dumped her backpack than someone would say, "Hey you have perfect pitch, what pitch is *this*?" and they'd knock their knuckles on the cover of their theory textbook or the shell of their violin case. Or a drummer would stroll up, sit down, and start tapping his hands on his thighs—bad enough, even before he turned to Enid and said, "Can you do that? Triplets in one hand and quarter notes on the other? Dude. Watch." Enid was a pianist, so of course she could do that; she'd mastered that in fifth grade, but she never said so.

Enid opened her notebook just as the music began: a steady buzz, a single sound building in intensity, until it broke. Then the tone resumed, but fuzzier. It sounded, Enid thought, like when you brushed long wet hair and pulled too hard and a hair snapped and curled on itself. She didn't write that; she wrote *tremolo*. She looked around the room as if she would spot the things she was listening for—harmony, melody. She wrote *crescendo*. No one else seemed to be writing much, though the composers were nodding along groovily with the noise. Enid wrote *decrescendo*.

Then: interesting sounds. Human sounds. A puff of air from pursed lips. A deep-throated scoffing. These came not from the record player but from the girl with the braid. She stood suddenly and turned, stomping up the side aisle toward the exit. Her blouse was a vintage number, all lace and tucks, and it was stuffed into the waistband of a thick skirt, too long and full to be fashionable, even in proto-Goth, late-grunge '96. The shoes might have been lug-soled boots like Enid's own Doc Martens, but Enid couldn't see them within the folds of the girl's skirt, could only hear her heavy footfalls. The girl swept past Enid's row, muttering something under her breath. Enid turned to watch her go, but she was the only one who did. As she turned back to her notebook, Enid saw the heads of her classmates fixed on the recital hall stage, or up at the ceiling, or down into laps, or on Dr. Doyle himself.

The music was still playing, a fat, complicated texture that didn't so much go anywhere as hover, intermittently loud. *Like a heavy flag flapping on a flagpole, momentarily still and then suddenly agitated, but static,* Enid wrote. Then she wrote, *bees.*

Enid would have liked to follow the strange girl, to find out where she'd come from and why she'd left so abruptly, but she had to get to Composing Seminar. All music majors had to take the core theory courses, but Composing Seminar with Dr. Hockbein was just for theory/comp majors, designed to be a kind of laboratory complement to the lectures. For the most part, the assignments in Composing Seminar were plausibly aligned with the corresponding theory courses: in previous semesters, they'd written string-quartet sketches, brief arias, romances, rondos, and variations on themes. It was in Composing Seminar that Enid felt simultaneously like a composer and not like a composer at all. Until they'd gotten to twentieth-century theory, the assignments themselves had been wonderful: opportunities to transfer book-and-lecture learning to manuscript paper, and to sound. To make music. To *compose*! But in a classroom with just the composers, Enid felt her differentness, her aloneness, her femaleness, acutely.

For this composing assignment in the seminar, aleatory, students were to experiment with the techniques in randomness—*Ah, ah that's Indeterminism*, Dr. Hockbein chided—pioneered by John Cage. Dr.

Hockbein asked the students to pair up and compare progress. "You're setting a text, but you're only going to be able to use a short fragment of the text," Dr. Hockbein explained, "so I want you to help each other choose your fragment. Try not to use *prettiness* as your guide, OK?" (Did he look pointedly at Enid when he said that?) "Don't pick based on what you like or what you think quote-unquote 'sounds good.' Remember the idea that words are just sound objects, not meaning-makers, OK?"

By the time Enid dug out her source text—a poem she'd hand-copied from a book—from her backpack, everyone had paired up except for Colin Carrasco. The music teachers loved Colin, the star of the composing program and the first-ever undergrad chair of the Contemporary Music Society, but the other composers seemed to like him even less than they liked Enid.

"Guess it's you and me," Colin said from across the classroom. He didn't make a move, so Enid dragged her desk over to his.

"Do you want to talk about yours first?" Enid asked. He didn't have his source text out. His desk was clear.

"No, let's see what you're working with." He reached for the poem Enid had written out, laying it out in front of him, arms folded across his chest, and began to read.

"Should I look at yours while you're doing that?"

He shook his head. An observer would have thought that Colin was a grad student and Enid a visitor to office hours, not that they were peers, the two least-liked members of the undergraduate composing program, partnered off by default.

He scanned the poem quickly.

"OK, so daddy issues," he said.

"Excuse me?"

"Just, yeah, I see how it fits with your whole, like, *thing*."

"My thing?"

"Yeah, the angry chick thing."

He couldn't have read much past the second stanza, past *Big as a Frisco seal*.

"You think this poem is about 'daddy issues?'" Enid asked.

"It's not a bad poem, though, from what I've read."

"I mean, yeah, it's Sylvia Plath. Wait, you think my thing is 'angry chick?'" Even if it were her "thing," how would Colin know? Enid kept her thoughts to herself. She barely spoke at school.

"I don't mean it like it's bad. At least you have a point of view. Me and you are like the only people in this program who have one," he whispered, as if the other pairs were paying them any attention.

"What's yours?"

"I'm Chilean."

"So your point of view is 'Chilean,' and mine is 'angry chick?'" If Enid was trying to persuade Colin that she had a different point of view, this wasn't going to help. She could feel her throat tightening.

"No, I mean, I get it," Colin said. "I know you think we all ignore you, but I heard what you were saying the other day about our visiting composer series."

At the last meeting of the Contemporary Music Society, Enid had finally spoken her mind. In a quavering voice, she had asked if the program could find a woman composer to invite to campus. "Who did you have in mind?" Dr. Doyle had asked, and Enid didn't have an answer, because she didn't actually know of any woman composers. It's not like they could invite Fanny Mendelssohn or Clara Schumann or Hildegard von Bingen, the only three who'd been so much as mentioned in class. But Colin, who fancied himself a super-enlightened statesman, and who never met a silence he didn't want to fill, said, "Here's an idea, why don't you do a little research, make a wish list, and if they're serious composers, you know, I'm totally down." He looked around at the other composers, at Dr. Doyle, who shrugged and said, "Sure."

"So, did you get a chance to do like I said?" Colin asked now, fingering a phantom keyboard on the poem on his desk.

Enid leaned down to her backpack and pulled out the textbook they used for the twentieth-century music history class. She'd felt so smart in her reasoning that any women she found in the required text would pass Colin's "seriousness" test, but when she put the book on his desk, she realized that the four measly Post-it notes clustered toward the end of the 400-page book looked pretty sad. "Here's a few ideas," she said, as Colin started flipping through.

"I'll check them out. No promises." He leaned back in his desk and dug a folded piece of notebook paper from the front pocket of his jeans. "Here's my source text."

Enid unfolded the square of paper and read:

> ANTS ARE SO FASCINATING
> By Colin Ricardo Reyes Carrasco
> (*after Pablo Neruda*)
>
> Ants are so fascinating
> That I let them climb all over my sandwich.
> They are smart, ambitious, mechanical,
> soldiers that take it all in stride.

"You wrote this?" Enid asked.

"An original," Colin said. "I mean, like it says, it's an homage to Neruda."

"This is—you have a lot of names," Enid said.

"Yeah, that's part of my thing. My middle name is actually Benjamin, but I'm alluding to how Neruda changed his own name. See? When you read poetry, you have to think of everything. Even the title is part of it."

"Clever," Enid said. In her own backpack was a promising paper she'd written about poetry, generously marked with her teacher's green scrawl. She hadn't officially changed her major (it was hard to stop trying to be the thing you'd always wanted to be, even if you no longer wanted to be it), but each semester, more and more of the classes on her schedule were chosen from the English department section of the course catalog. Her backpack was a heavy jumble of mixed prose and poems and letters and novels and stories and criticism, crowding out her sheet music, manuscript paper, and theory textbooks.

"Thanks."

Dr. Hockbein called the students back. Enid took her poem and her desk back to her side of the room. For the rest of the class, while Dr. Hockbein told the class what criteria to use to select their text fragments, Enid reread "Daddy." She knew two things: For her composition, she wanted to use *in the freakish Atlantic / where it pours bean green over blue*. And she'd chosen it because it was pretty, so she knew that she was not serious.

When Composing Seminar was over, Enid was grateful for a good reason to avoid lingering at the Smoking Section. She went up to the music library, found a study carrel near the back, and laid out her stuff for her aleatoric composing assignment. When she'd first decided she wanted to be a composer, in the third grade after watching *Amadeus*, the tools she'd pictured using were inkpots, creamy staff paper, and a candelabra perched on a piano, not blank white paper, pencils, a straight edge. She dug a lint-encrusted 800mg ibuprofen pill out of her bag and put it on the table. Enid had been having headaches all semester, and she didn't know if they were attributable to dehydration, Colin Carrasco, or a steady diet of atonal music.

She finished taking all the measurements she needed from the dots and line segments scattered across the page, lost in almost-mathematical concentration, and when she looked up, the girl with the braid was standing there in front of her. Straight on, Enid could see her face was heart-shaped, with large brown eyes behind those wire glasses and unruly brows sloping slightly at the sides. Her long dark hair had come loose from its thick braid and was hanging to her collarbone—or where Enid guessed her collarbone was behind the pin-tucked fabric of her weird high-necked blouse. Her arms hung at her sides, her hands empty. She stood uncomfortably close to Enid, staring.

"Uh, hi," Enid said. Where was her backpack, her instrument?

"You can see me." It was a question or a statement, or something in between.

"Well, you're right there. Do I know you?"

"I don't think so," the girl said. "Do you?"

"No. I mean, I saw you this morning, in Dr. Doyle's class. Where are you from?"

"Ohio," she said. "Originally."

"I've never seen you before this morning."

The girl picked up one of Enid's pencils and rolled it between her palms, never breaking her gaze. "Where did *you* come from?"

"Maryland. Did you just get here?"

"Maryland! I live there. Do you know Pomeroy?"

"The conservatory? Yeah. Everybody—"

"I rather love it there." She didn't have an accent exactly, but an errant Britishness popped up here and there: *rah-ther*.

When Enid was growing up, the state music teachers' association hosted annual piano competitions at Pomeroy the first weekend in May. Enid loved it, too: the tights and patent leather shoes and special dresses the day called for; how the shoes sounded on Baltimore's grimy sidewalks and the polished tile floors and grand spiral staircase; the thick-glassed windows with the old-timey metal radiators; the creaking chairs and gleaming statues; the grandmotherly smells of the carpet, the drapes. And she loved the fistfuls of satin prize ribbons she brought home each time. When the time came to apply for college, though, Enid knew she wasn't a conservatory-caliber pianist or composer. She missed those annual visits to Pomeroy, or she missed the girl in tights and patent leather shoes who didn't yet know she was only a state-college-caliber musician. If that. "You go to Pomeroy?" Enid reconsidered the girl's outfit. Maybe grunge was playing out really differently in Baltimore. "What do you play?"

"Viola," she said. She put the pencil back on Enid's desk. "Mainly. Also piano. But I'm a composer. Well, I will be." She used one long finger to spin the paper toward her. "What is this?"

"Composing homework, actually. I'm a theory/comp major too."

"This is your composition?" She wrinkled her nose, though Enid wasn't sure if it was a reaction to the composition or just a way to push her glasses back up without using her hands, a skill most glasses-wearing musicians had to master.

"Yeah, I mean, not my own music; it's a thing we have to do for Dr. Hockbein."

"An exercise."

"Exactly. It's aleatory." Enid couldn't believe that her state school was ahead of Pomeroy in its curriculum. "You haven't done aleatory yet?"

"No," she said. "What is it?"

"It's the whole leave-it-up-to-chance thing. It can be, you know, using dice or something to assign random pitches or duration. Like Cage."

"Cage?"

"John Cage. You don't study Cage?"

"No," she said. "Dice?"

Enid thought of all the years she'd spent wishing she had a shot at Pomeroy.

"Yeah. He used the I Ching to make his decisions, so we're supposed to use the principles of aleatory in our own way. I'm using this text." Enid passed the girl the hand-copied poem.

"Is this you then—are you Sylvia?"

"What? No, I'm not *Sylvia Plath*," Enid laughed. She wondered if she needed to alert whoever was in charge of those college rankings at *U.S. News and World Report*. Pomeroy!

"Is she a composer too?"

"No. Yes. No. She's a poet. Was. She's dead. You mean you've never heard of Sylvia Plath?" Enid's mother had warned her that a conservatory education wasn't well-rounded, but in what universe did a girl who went around dressed like *this* not go through a *Bell Jar* phase? "Why did you say, 'You can see me?'"

"I've been walking up and down these corridors, and you're the only person who's said so much as hello. I'm invisible here, it seems."

"Tell me about it," Enid said.

"So how do you play this?"

"I don't know. I'm just going to get all my measurements and write it out and turn it in. It doesn't matter what it sounds like. That's not the point."

"What could be more 'the point' than the sound of music?"

Enid laughed, but the girl didn't. "Let me guess, you've never heard of *The Sound of Music* either. To answer your question, I just have to measure each of these lines using this pill and then whatever the number is, that tells me what pitch—sorry, pitch class—and how long to hold it. And then I've assigned each of the words of my text a number, too, and so, that's . . . that."

Enid hated this. She didn't want to think about music like this. She never wanted to write a sentence like, *The cells are intervallically related in the relative closeness of the second pitch of the cell to the first, i.e., most are 0-1, or 0-2, only F and G are larger: 0-4*, as she had on a recent test, in response to which she had gotten marked off two points because, according to Dr. Doyle, $D=inv.\ subset\ of\ G\ and\ A = inv.\ subset\ of\ E$. Ordinarily, being dinged two points on a music assignment would have stung. But if this was music, Enid struggled to care about it or the deducted points.

"But where did they come from? The lines and the dots?"

"This is just how it's supposed to be, OK? Trust me. You'll see when you get to Cage." Enid's eyes went swimmy looking at her work in progress. She couldn't remember where the dots and lines had come from. Had she dropped the pill from a height of six feet and marked its landings? The only thing that made sense to her was the fragment of text, and even that had been brutalized into non-meaning in her hands.

"This is music?"

"Like I said, it's an assignment."

"It's clever, I suppose. But do you *like* this music?"

Just then, Colin Carrasco came around the corner. "There you are." He didn't look at the girl with the braid. "OK, Joan Tower's the real deal," he said, putting the book down on top of Enid's composition and opening to the first sticky on page 171. "But no way we can afford her. Same goes for Pauline Oliveros," as he flipped to the second sticky on page 308. "And this—Robin Mortimore? I never heard of her." Then he was at the last sticky, on page 317. "Laurie... Anderson," he said as his eyes scanned the short paragraph. "This one's gonna be a no, I think." He looked up at Enid. "What? Look." He turned the book around so Enid could read it, though she knew exactly what it said. Laurie Anderson was described as a "performance artist," whose work was somewhere between popular and serious. Such meager choices, Enid thought for the thousandth time since coming to college to study music. Popular *or* serious. "Bummer," Colin said.

"So two of them are too famous, and two of them are not famous enough?"

"One of those isn't even a real composer," Colin said. "Laurie. She's like an *actress*. Pauline and Joan are cool, no idea about Rachel or whatever."

"Robin. *Mortimore*," Enid added, because that's how you talk about composers: Cage and Reich, not John and Steve.

"Listen," Colin said then. "I feel for you. Seriously. I get it. There are no other Chileans in this program, either. It's lonely. But I think you have to do what I do, and just use your imagination."

"My—"

"Like, just because none of the invited composers has been Chilean doesn't mean I can't picture myself as a composer, right? Like that. Whoever visits, when they talk about their work and their life, I just," he tapped his temple, "transpose it to Chilean in my mind. Imagination."

The girl with the braid watched Colin go, then turned back to Enid. "A wisenheimer, that one." Odd as she was, she was a quick study.

"Yeah. He's a dick."

Enid wondered if she should explain this vulgarity to her new friend, but her pink cheeks said she'd taken the meaning.

"I asked him to invite some women composers to visit, and—well, you heard him. It's impossible."

"Why should that be impossible?"

"There aren't women composers, I guess. They don't exist."

"I exist. You exist. That's two in this room," the girl said. "Though, if I may say so . . ." She looked down at Enid's aleatory assignment.

"Don't bother," Enid said. "I know."

"And what about your classmates? There were plenty of girls in that seminar this morning, with Dr. So-and-So and his dreadful noise machine."

"Not composers. All performers. I'm the only one, if that's what you're asking."

"The only one!"

"What, is it different at Pomeroy?"

"I'll say. We have so many girls studying composition that they had to hire a teacher from England just for us. That's Langdon. Why, there's Ebbe, and Hermine, and Katharine, and dear old Psyche, of course—oh!—and Adelheid gave her diploma concert last November —an entire program of her compositions. There was a piano quintet, and a pair of vocal quartets, and—"

"Hermine? Adelheid? *Psyche?*"

"Yes, and oh, her songs! Our very own Schubert, Adelheid is."

"Well, here it's just me," Enid sighed. She loved Schubert and the name Psyche. If she was going to have an old-timey name, why couldn't her mother have picked that one?

"Well, I can't see as it matters whether music is written by a man or a woman if it's any good. Anyhow, Adelheid's program has me thinking. I should like to have some songs on my diploma concert when the time comes—it's not for some time yet, you see, I still have to complete my studies and my examinations, and that means I've still got eight-voice fugues ahead of me, and of course we're to complete an overture for full orchestra, and, well, as I've said, I've only just begun as a composer, really. Langdon says—"

"Who's Langdon again?"

"Luther Langdon? My teacher! Our teacher, I should say. He's quite notable." The girl took a seat and settled backward into her chair, letting her eyes roam the library while her mouth chattered on. "Whenever I get fearful about all the difficult things that lie ahead in my studies, he tells me to play my viola—run off and play now, dear girl, he says, he does love to tease me—but it's always just the thing. When I was struggling with double counterpoint, he stopped my lesson and asked if I might like to play with him. We did the Vieuxtemps Sonata in B-flat—do you know that one?—just the second movement, the Andante. Langdon was so clumsy with the piano part, but we kept at it. It was dusk when I left his office, but wouldn't you know it? The next morning I knew just how to complete my counterpoint!"

Enid had taken modal counterpoint as well, the previous school year. She had also found all the rules mind-meltingly difficult. But she was stubborn, and she liked crossword puzzles, and those turned out to be what she needed to ace it. By the midpoint of the semester, she'd established herself as the best in the class. Dr. Roderick, the youngest member of the composing faculty, a handsome, thick-haired man who ditched the professorial sport coat in favor of candy-striped Polo shirts, and who smiled more frequently than the rest of the sour faculty combined, would call on her whether she raised her hand or not, and when he slid her graded tests back onto her desk he left them face-up, with large circled As, and would say, winking, "Very nice again, Enid."

Across the curriculum—a battery of music theory and history classes the music majors marched through in lockstep—students were immersed in the eighteenth- and nineteenth-century music that they had been weaned on, through years of private lessons, honors orchestras, and school bands: the lush and pompous and sentimental and perfectly sense-making music of major-minor keys that, even when stretched to within an inch of its life by heartbreaking, nearly ear-splitting chromaticism, always resolved. The early music of that counterpoint class was exotic—Enid had never listened to Palestrina—but it was a spooky-holy predecessor of the church music that moved her to tears, even though she wasn't a believer. Enid sometimes wondered if her initial error of establishing herself as the best in her class at old, dead music was why no one seemed to take her very seriously as a composer now: current, original, alive.

"Who are you?" she asked the odd, out-of-nowhere girl-composer.

The girl leaned forward and extended her long right hand to Enid. "Gloria Clifford," she said. Her grip was strong and firm.

"Enid Bluff." Her head was pounding and she was desperate to head back to her on-campus studio "apartment." Most days, Enid could go without having a full-fledged conversation with anyone; even so, music school days were loud with Dr. Wallace's tests, Dr. Doyle's modern music artifacts, the endless compositional directives of Dr. Hockbein, the interstitial chatter of Colin Carrasco, the gossip and cackling and competition of the Smoking Section, and the aural litter spilling from practice rooms and mixing noxiously in hallways. Enid depended on her cold, spartan cinder-block dorm (an "apartment" because it had its own permanently grimy bathroom and the faintest hint of a kitchen, with a mini-fridge, a bar sink, and an ancient two-burner stove) as a sanctuary. In the evenings, she lay on her twin bed in the quiet, letting her brain empty of the day's noise, and then, after the hottest shower she could coax out of the pipes, she did her reading or assignments for the English courses that were slowly but surely wooing her away from the music school. When she got into bed, she let her three-CD changer refill her head and body with reassuring musics—each night, an eclectic three-course meal: Tori, Schubert, Björk; Chopin, Jewel, Bach; Fiona, Piazzolla, Madonna. "I need to get going here," she said, packing her unfinished composition into her overfull backpack along with her history book and its four unsuitable women. She was beginning to like this weird, chatty stranger. But her poor head. "I'll see you if you're around tomorrow."

"Tomorrow," Gloria said, standing now from the upholstered library chair and walking toward the window. "Before you go, though, I wonder if you might be able to point me to some scores or sheet music. This is the library, is it not?"

"Oh, yeah. Sure. Stacks are that way. You can search what you're looking for there." Enid pointed out the computer station, its little box of scrap paper and golf pencils beside.

"I think I'll browse," Gloria said, looking warily at the computer and instead walking in the direction of the rows and rows of bookshelves, all densely packed with solid-color, hardbound editions, each spine embossed with the composer's name in white capital letters.

"You're not going to be able to check anything out, though," Enid called after her, but Gloria disappeared into the stacks, skirt rustling. What do I know? Enid thought. Maybe Pomeroy students get borrowing privileges at any music library in the world.

Back in her cinderblock chamber that night, Enid took her hot shower and then, towel still on her head, went to the twenty-volume paperback encyclopedia of music and musicians that her mother had bought her as a graduation gift. It was an expensive gift, especially for a single mother, but it was perfect for a kid who, as a third grader, had asked for staff paper and calligraphy pens from Santa Claus. Facing this $500 investment in the form of twenty handsome bright-blue books in a row, Enid was ashamed to be flaming out of even this music school. She wanted to look up the viola sonata Gloria had mentioned playing with her teacher. Remembering only that it started with V, she grabbed Vols. 20 (Virelai to Żywny) and 19 (Tiomkin to Virdung). When she found Vieuxtemps (violin virtuoso and composer born in Belgium in 1820, notable exponent of the Franco-Belgian school of violin, died of a stroke in 1881) she jotted a note to herself to check out a CD of the B-flat sonata from the music library. Then, she sat on the floor beside her bookshelf and browsed the twenty volumes and visited old friends: hello, Khachatourian, howdy, Szymanowski. On her way to visit old Wanda Landowska, Enid was leafing through Vol. 10 (Kern to Lindelheim) when, on the very same page she'd visited so many times, she spotted a puzzling entry:

LANGDON, LUTHER (b. 1871, Harrow, U.K.; d.1958, Baltimore, Md.). Composer, pianist, librettist. Best known for his modern opera EEPERSIP (1938), based on the sensational 1927 novel *The House Without Windows* by child prodigy Barbara Newhall Follett, whose mysterious disappearance is thought by some to have inspired not only LANGDON's magnum opus but also the 1940 disappearance of Langdon's own wife, composer CLIFFORD, GLORIA. From 1908 to his death, LANGDON served as professor of theory and composition at POMEROY CONSERVATORY, Baltimore, Md., where he launched the career of composer HOBART, PSYCHE.

Even as she read the entry on Langdon and tried to fashion a full story out of its clues, to square it with the account she'd heard from the chatty girl in the music library, in Enid's mind there was a whisper of doubt, a tiny voice that told her she had imagined—perhaps hallucinated—Gloria. The whisper said that her exchange with the girl in the library had been, at best, some benign manifestation of stress, at worst, the opening overtures of a crackup.

She rifled through the volumes spread out on her floor until she came to Vol. 4 (Castrucci to Courante) and flipped through the pages so fast she nearly ripped a few from the binding. Toward the end of the volume, she had it:

CLIFFORD, GLORIA (b. 1890, Dayton, Ohio; d.?). Composer, violist. Wife and muse of LANGDON, LUTHER, who was her teacher at POMEROY CONSERVATORY. Best known for a handful of chamber works, including her dazzling SONATA FOR VIOLA AND PIANO (1919). Disappeared abruptly in 1940, when she is presumed to have died, though her death has never been confirmed. The general quality of her compositions, as well as the irresistible prurience of the circumstances surrounding the mysterious end of her life, made her a stalwart of the viola repertoire, especially for young players.

Several of the books lay open on the floor around Enid, with Vols. 10 and 4 on top of the pile, each open to its confusing revelation. The entries for Luther Langdon and Gloria Clifford had black-and-white photos, which she studied even as the towel dropped from her head, even as her untended wet hair dripped down the back of her T-shirt. So much of what she read lined up with what the girl in the library said. Gloria Clifford was a composer, significant enough to be included in the encyclopedia. Luther Langdon was her teacher at Pomeroy.

In Langdon's picture, he was seated in front of a piano, as if he'd just been playing when a photographer to his right called his name, prompting him to rotate his body to the camera. His left elbow was propped on the instrument, his large, elegant left hand cupping his ear. His right arm rested in his lap. He was wearing a lot of clothes, Enid noted: a wide-lapeled jacket; a crisp white shirt with a rounded collar; a pale, perfectly knotted tie tucked into a vest. His light hair was meticulously parted and combed to the side. He had a deep philtrum and a chin dimple, two oddities that had the effect of drawing attention to the sexiest mouth Enid had ever seen in a historical photo of a dead person.

In her picture, Gloria had dark hair parted in the middle that fell in wide, crimpy waves to her cheekbones. She wore a dark dress and a short strand of dark beads around her neck. She jutted out her chin. She looked up and slightly to the left of the lens. She looked about thirty and wasn't wearing her glasses, but the face was—indisputably—the face of the girl Enid had been with in the library that afternoon.

Before that morning, when Gloria turned up in the lecture, Enid had never heard of her. She supposed it was possible to imagine something you'd never heard of, but how to explain the factual accuracy of her imagination? How to explain that everything Gloria had told her was turning out to be true? What, she wondered, was the connection between Luther Langdon, *The House Without Windows*, and Gloria Clifford? Was it, as the encyclopedia implied, that Gloria had found—would find—inspiration for her own disappearance in the author's disappearance, and Langdon, in turn, found the inspiration for his opera in his wife's vanishing? Then there was the matter of Gloria and Psyche Hobart, whom Enid recognized from the long list of Gloria's fellow composers—both of them Langdon's students, one of whom he mentored and the other he married. One who lived, and one who vanished forever. Enid had no idea how or why Gloria had been picked up out of 1910 Baltimore and deposited in Arizona in 1996, but her inability to explain the mechanics, Enid found, didn't prevent her from wanting to believe the situation. It didn't prevent her from believing she had just met Gloria Clifford.

On Thursday morning, Enid's aleatory assignment sat unfinished in the bottom of her backpack throughout her two morning classes, The 19th-Century British Novel (which the TA had them calling "Baggy Monsters") and Confessional Poetry (the TA in that class did not make jokes), both held on the other side of campus in the English department. She didn't make it back to the music building until after lunch, and then she had a piano lesson.

Dr. Barton-Aster put her through her paces on the Schubert sonata she was working on. They spent most of the sixty minutes working on the slow second movement, which Enid loved but couldn't keep from dragging. Dr. Barton-Aster stood next to the piano, just out of Enid's peripheral vision, making big sweeping circles with her short, fat arms, as if the piano were the sea and the sonata a boat without oars, and she was trying to propel Enid back to shore.

At the end of the lesson, as Enid was putting the Schubert back in her backpack, she waited for a break in Dr. Barton-Aster's monologue—"Remember: you want loooooooong, unbroken lines, but you must actually connect the notes; you can't use the damper pedal to do the hard work for you"—so she could ask, as casually as possible:

"Have you ever heard of Gloria Clifford?"

"Well, of course, dear. Why do you ask?"

"I just—" Enid began. "I hadn't—I ran into—" She couldn't finish her sentence, even though she knew, raised on *Back to the Future* movies and a time-travel TV show called *Voyagers!*, that the Gloria she'd been with in the library—a real girl with frizzed hair and sweat rings on her cotton blouse—was indeed the vanished woman pictured in the music encyclopedia. Younger, but the same person. She was visiting from Pomeroy Conservatory, visiting from another time, it was as simple as that. It was (what was the term she'd learned on the other side of campus?) the donnée. But she also knew she couldn't say any of that to her piano teacher without getting a swift referral to the Student Health Center.

"Such a shame. She's probably the best woman composer America has ever produced. Or could have been, anyway."

"Why don't we study her then?" On this familiar topic, Enid felt pricklier than usual. It was no longer an abstract question. It was personal.

"Oh, who knows?" Dr. Barton-Aster sighed. "She wrote mostly for viola, mostly smaller forms, chamber music. She never wrote anything truly big. She could have, though. She could have been an American Debussy."

"What happened to her?" In music school, as in the music encyclopedia, the life of any composer was kept to a three-note structure, a broken triad: When was he born? What is he known for? When did he die? Enid knew the question would come out of her mouth and land on Dr. Barton-Aster's ears as an academic one, that of an earnest student eager to master a new topic. But Enid was not asking for the three notes that made up Gloria's story, which she already knew: Gloria composed, she married, she disappeared. What she hoped Dr. Barton-Aster could provide was the space between the notes, the silences that made the sounds meaningful.

"No one really knows. In any case, she didn't live long enough to fulfill her potential. But the work there is, well, it's just lovely. See you next week, dear."

It was half past two when Enid left her piano lesson and set out to find Gloria. She looked through the open doors of each classroom she passed, in the stairwells up and down, at the Smoking Section, in the tiny windows of the closet-sized practice rooms along the corridor to the library. She wanted to compare notes with Gloria, to find out what she knew about how she'd gotten here. And if it felt right, and if Gloria wanted, she could show her the books in her backpack, the dog-eared entries on Gloria Clifford and Luther Langdon, her teacher and husband-to-be.

Enid also had to finish the damned aleatory assignment that was due the next day, so she went back to the music library where maybe, she thought, Gloria would be waiting for her at the study carrel where they'd first spoken. But when she found the carrels empty, she felt too disappointed to work on the assignment. Instead, she went to the library computer stand, intending to look up the Vieuxtemps so she could check out a recording and a score of the piece that had formed the soundtrack of Gloria's relationship with Langdon. She grabbed a scrap of paper and a golf pencil but then, impulsively, she typed *Gloria Clifford* into the search box. When the computer blinked up a page of results—the very same picture on the screen that was in the volume weighing down her backpack—Enid felt none of the dizzy disorientation she'd felt as she plowed through the encyclopedias the night before. Instead, she felt the solid comfort of recognition. *There she is*, she thought. *My friend.*

Enid wrote down the locations of all the library's holdings directly or indirectly related to Gloria Clifford. She found the Vieuxtemps score and a CD recording by someone named Bruno Giuranna. She found the score of Gloria's 1919 *Sonata for Viola and Piano*, but no recordings. She even found a whole album of works by Psyche Hobart—she couldn't wait to make sure Colin Carrasco saw that, though she was pretty sure they couldn't invite Psyche Hobart to campus (born in 1890 in Indiana; composed mostly for voice; known as one of the "ultramoderns"; died in Philadelphia in 1972)—and she found the score and a recording of Langdon's great opera *Eepersip*. As for the book that inspired it, *The House Without Windows*, she'd have to go to the main stacks in the center of campus. As Enid left the music library, arms full of research, she passed Dr. Hockbein coming in.

"Hello, Enid," he said.

"Hi, Dr. Hockbein," Enid said, her heavy backpack pulling on her spine, her arms aching. "Have you ever heard of Gloria Clifford?"

"Someone's been poking around under dusty doilies in the library I see," Dr. Hockbein said, peering over his glasses at the bounty Enid clutched to her chest. "What brings up Gloria Clifford, of all things?"

"Do you think she could have been another Debussy?"

Dr. Hockbein laughed. "Where'd you get that idea?"

"Dr. Barton-Aster said."

"Oh, well, I can see why she'd say that, I suppose."

"What do you mean?" As Enid questioned her teacher, she realized something had shifted in her with the discovery of Gloria Clifford. She wasn't asking Dr. Hockbein about her because she thought he knew something she didn't; she was teasing out the holes in his knowledge. *She* was testing *him*.

"Listen, Enid. Gloria Clifford was a passable chamber-music writer. But the only reason anyone talks about her anymore is because of this new, very fashionable interest in women composers, and because of all the . . . tragedy around her. It's made her a favorite of odd, maudlin girls. You're not going to fall in with that crowd, are you?"

That Dr. Hockbein didn't already consider her an odd, maudlin girl felt like a compliment to Enid. "No, I was just wondering. What tragedy? Her disappearance?"

"And the whole thing with her father, she's just a sad old figure, start to finish."

Enid did not know how or why Gloria disappeared, but she did know that Gloria was not a sad figure. She was odd, cheerful, occasionally cocky. Hockbein was failing her quiz. "What whole thing?"

"Oh, let's see if I can remember how it goes: happy little rich girl worships her father, he sends her off to Pomeroy, he dies, she marries her professor so she can maintain her lifestyle."

"Her lifestyle—as a composer?"

"Oh, she never composed much after that. Strike that—I guess there was a big sonata. Yes, I see you've got it there. Anyway, after that, Langdon kept her in corsets or shoes or somesuch. I'll tell you what, though, his work only got better after . . . well, of course you've heard his *Eepersip*."

Enid gestured down at the clutch of books and CDs in her arms. "Not yet," she said. "But I've got it here."

"Good. Now, what about you? How's your assignment coming? Have you chosen a text?"

"Oh, that. Yeah. I'm using a part of a Sylvia Plath poem."

Dr. Hockbein sighed. "You know, I never forgave Sylvia Plath for killing herself."

"You like poetry?"

"Well, of course. More of a Berryman fan, really. With Plath, it's—

every halfway smart girl I met in college thought she had to want to put her head in an oven to be taken seriously. If you like Plath, Enid, you really need to read some Berryman. Check out *Dream Songs*. Now *that's* poetry."

It was almost four o'clock when Enid made it down to the Smoking Section, desperate to find Gloria chattering the ear off of some miserable jazz pianist. But she wasn't there. Enid checked the harpsichord studio, half-expecting to find an Early Music grad student taking a break from hand-carving his crumhorn reed to flirt with this female specimen refreshingly unaware of *Friends*, Radiohead, or trousers.

But Gloria was nowhere to be found. Enid dreaded returning alone to her apartment, dreaded finishing her composing assignment. She had other homework she could do—counterpoint, history, some reading for Baggy Monsters—but none of it appealed. Enid headed for one of the practice rooms on the first floor: Gloria's advice (Langdon's, really) seemed right. Maybe if she planted herself somewhere obvious and played the right music, she could make Gloria appear.

In a practice room on the first floor, she put her library books and CDs on the lid of the piano and dumped her backpack on the floor, zipped tight, Schubert shut up inside. Suddenly unburdened of all that weight, she almost felt like she was levitating. She shook out her tired arms and hands. She didn't want to practice; she wanted to play. She opened the fallboard of the piano and let her memory, stored not so much in her mind as in her hands, guide her. They reached for the first bars of a Bach invention in B-flat: left hand moving in orderly eighth notes through broken major triads (the I, the IV) while the right hand produced a singable melody in sixteenths. She was headed into the imitative section, left hand calling to right, right answering, when she heard a third, then a fourth voice echoing the phrases through the walls.

Adam.

Enid had failed to ensure that the practice room she chose wasn't next to Adam's. No matter what you were playing, he would play it back to you twice as fast and three times as loud, and then he would spin it off into his own ridiculous variation of your music, swinging it, shifting it to minor, adding an Alberti bass, making it a waltz, adding Lisztian octaves tramping all over. The first time she'd experienced Adam, she'd tried shifting to one of her own compositions, figuring it would stymie him. It did not. She received her own musical ideas back to her through the walls with the Asshole Mozart treatment. Enid stopped playing and sat at the piano. If you waited him out, he went away.

Once Adam had gone—the room creaked, his door slammed, his shadow crossed the small window in her door—Enid reached for the score for Gloria Clifford's *Sonata for Viola and Piano* that she'd checked out from the music library. On the first page, just opposite Gloria Clifford's name, was a snippet of a poem in French; Enid would work that out later, with her dictionary. The music was printed on three staves, the viola line floating above the double staff of the piano part. For the first page of the first movement, the piano didn't do more than hold onto some great big chords while the viola announced itself, so Enid kept her hands still on the keyboard and sight-sung the viola part, at least until it shifted to alto clef. Things got more interesting for the pianist at the top of the second page, where there was a meter change, a new tempo marking—*poco agitato*—and some tricky triplets-against-eighths to deal with.

The fifth and sixth pages of the first movement had a lush chromatic solo for the piano while the viola rested, and that's what Enid was working through—tongue poking out in concentration—when Gloria Clifford opened the door of the practice room.

"Now *that* is lovely," she said. "Is that one of your own?"

"No," Enid said, turning from the piano, relieved and delighted at the familiar face and voice. "It's you."

"It is I," Gloria said, giving a theatrical curtsy, one long arm flung into the air. In the other arm she held a hardshell viola case. She smiled at Enid. She was wearing the same voluminous skirt and boots, the same pin-tucked blouse. Depending on how long she was planning to stay, Gloria might need to make a run over to Buffalo Exchange.

"I was looking for you," Enid said, as Gloria set the case on the floor and snapped its clasps open.

"I've been looking for you, too," Gloria said. She lifted the instrument from its case and began tuning it, rosining her bow.

"How did you get here?" Enid asked. "And, um, did you gank someone's viola?"

Gloria looked down at the instrument and shrugged. "I did not . . . *gank*. I've just been wandering about. This is a very strange place. As for the instrument, it was unattended. I've only borrowed it."

"I mean, how did you get . . . here."

"Oh. Yes. That." Gloria nodded, which confirmed that she took the meaning. "I've been wanting to discuss this with you as well. I'd know better how I got here if you could please tell me where I am, exactly?"

"Arizona," Enid said. "How old are you?"

"Arizona Territory!" Gloria said. "Imagine. Twenty. Well, nearly —Christmas."

"It's a state now," Enid said. "When are you—when were you born, like what year?"

"Ninety." Gloria looked around the dismal practice room. "And you?"

"Seventy-seven," Enid said. "Like, *nineteen* seventy-seven." Somewhere not too far from Baltimore, in Gloria's waking life, Enid's own grandmother was a newborn. "I'm twenty, too. Or I will be, in

March. Welcome to 1996, I guess?" The two women looked at one another for a long instant, during which they understood, and agreed on, the plain fact of the magic that joined them. They didn't need to discuss it when they could be enjoying it instead.

"Do you want to try this?" Enid asked, pointing to the score that sat open on the piano's music stand. Enid spun back around on the bench, put her hands on the keys.

Gloria stepped forward and took her position behind Enid's shoulder. "Let's go back to the beginning, shall we?"

Enid turned the pages until she got back to the top of the score. There, the poem in French. There, the composer's name.

She heard Gloria gasp. "It's—mine?"

"Yes. You start," Enid said quietly. "I don't come in until the second measure. I'll follow you."

Gloria played the sonata perfectly, and why wouldn't she? But even Enid played better than seemed possible; she caught every accidental, the enormous stacked chords fit neatly into her hands, she seemed to smell changes of meter or tempo or dynamics from three measures away, so she was ready when they materialized. They played through all three movements without speaking, not even employing the nearly telepathic half-utterances musicians use with one another—*should we go back to the, yes; let's take it from, OK, I'll give you two and the buh buh BUH*—because there was no need. The music was fully formed, intact, perfect. Enid and Gloria weren't making it; they were *in* it.

At the last measure, they hit their *fortississimo* doubled-octave E's—*secco*, no pedal for Enid, dry—and let the silence of the rest of the measure ring: three-and-a-half beats. Then, Gloria spoke. She pointed the tip of her bow at the bottom of the page. "Composed in 1919. I write that... nine years from now."

"Yes," Enid said, cheeks flaming as she thought of the books she had in her bag. No, she would not show Gloria what she looked like after writing the sonata. Her short hair and beaded necklace. Her sad eyes. She would not show her the picture of Langdon, whom she'd recognize as her teacher, but her husband? She would not tell Gloria how her life ends, not with the perfect authentic cadence of death and burial but with disappearance. With measures of silence trailing off into forever. Unresolved.

Enid could protect Gloria from learning, prematurely, about her fate, but who could say what effect this time-travel detour would have on Gloria's trajectory? Enid had debuted, in unspectacular sight-reading, Gloria Clifford's great viola sonata for Gloria Clifford herself. How would hearing her own compositions-to-come change things? And—spinning this out—what would happen if Enid played *The Rite of Spring* for Gloria? Would Gloria Clifford go back to 1910, an almost-twenty-year-old girl in a fussy blouse, and beat Stravinsky to the punch?

Enid shook the idea out of her head. "Do you want to eat?" she asked. "Are you hungry? I have a little kitchen." Enid didn't feel hungry, but she could tell it was getting late. Outside the practice room, the sky had turned a dazzling pink and orange. Enid closed the score and put it back on the stack on the lid of the piano. She slung her heavy backpack over one shoulder and scooped the books and CDs from the lid of the piano into her arms.

"I can't say I feel hungry," Gloria admitted. "And I'm afraid if I drink anything I'll—you know. I don't know if I'm in my full body. I'm still not sure but that I'm dreaming. But I want to see where you live. Shall we go?"

They exited the music building to find the sky a brilliant orange-red turning dusky at the edges. Enid decided not to tell Gloria that it was pollution that enabled this spectacular desert sunset, now closing out its final movement. They watched together in silence before starting out across the campus, dark and empty of the forty thousand students who'd crawled it hours before.

"Is this permitted?" Gloria asked as they started out from the music building and headed toward the fountain by the student union, where Enid knew they would find Richard, the skinny old man in hiking boots who sat there all day and every night, smoking a joint and picking an out-of-tune guitar for an audience of oil-black common grackles. Gloria looped her arm through Enid's and pulled close, as if frightened.

"Is what permitted? Walking?" Enid laughed sharply but loved Gloria's arm in her own, and hoped she would leave it there.

"Not *walking*, silly. Going about unchaperoned. After dark."

Enid shrugged. "It's not a big deal," she said, in a voice that sounded more carefree than she felt. The truth was, Enid didn't feel entirely comfortable crossing the dark campus all alone, either, but she talked herself out of it: there hadn't been any incidents on campus that she'd heard of, for one, and the conventional wisdom nowadays was that it wasn't strangers jumping out of bushes you really had to be afraid of, it was people you'd gone on dates with. It was unattended drinks at frat parties. Enid didn't go to frat parties.

Gloria eyed the man at the fountain warily as they passed, but Enid raised a hand in greeting. Richard was harmless, she knew, a living statue, the shapeshifting center of a miasma of pot smoke and legend. Every so often, the student newspaper sent a reporter to try to interview him, to settle the rumors: was he really a hobo, a professor, a genius, a physicist, a lawyer, a beatnik, a billionaire, a felon? Richard only ever smiled and asked the reporter if they had any weed. If anything, Enid found Richard's constant presence comforting, a momentary respite from any apprehension she felt about walking alone. Whatever else he was, he was a sentry, his BIC lighter a lantern.

They passed out of range of the fountain and onto the dark palm-lined walk that ended at her campus apartment. Enid's unease returned when they approached a small square of grass and a solitary Chinese elm. She was reminded, again, that her preparation for the dangers of college—mostly from *Sassy* magazine and a handful of girls-only assemblies in high school—had been inadequate, that strangers in bushes and unattended drinks at frat parties were only two items on a lengthy menu of things to be afraid of.

It was October of her freshman year, right before midterms. That evening, she'd been just out of the shower, lying on her bed in flannel pants and a ratty T-shirt, when her phone rang. "Hey, Enid?" the voice said. It was a man's voice, familiar but unplaceable.

"This is she," she said.

"*This is she!*" he said. "So proper. What's up, Enid?" He sounded like he was smiling. He sounded hot.

"Who is this?"

"It's me . . . Greg? From counterpoint?"

She couldn't place him. Was there a Greg in counterpoint? It was possible, among the many Daves and Jasons.

"Listen, I'm so fucking stuck on this assignment that's due tomorrow. Have you done it yet?"

"How did you get my number?" Was Greg the lanky drummer with untied sneakers and curls hanging over his gray eyes? Or was he the guitar player with the gap between his front teeth?

"I just, like, have no idea how to do this. Can you help me? I've been going in circles since . . ." His voice trailed away from the phone, then it came back full volume. "I thought, fuck this, I'm calling counterpoint girl."

"Counterpoint girl?"

"Come on, don't act like you don't know you're the only one in there who knows what the fuck is going on."

"No, I mean, I think it's hard, too." That was true. It was hard, but hard like a puzzle. She was never lost; she just kept working at it. "I had no clue how to do that last one," she lied. Whoever Greg was, she didn't want him to feel bad that modal counterpoint was giving him trouble.

"It is hard! *So hard*." He laughed. "But then you got an A. I saw that. So—like I said, counterpoint girl."

Was Greg the silent tuba player who sat behind her? Who never even looked at her? That would have enabled him to see her grade on her paper, but this voice—cheery, flirty?—didn't sound like the way that guy looked.

"So where are you stuck?"

"Oh, right. It's this—species thing. I got my exercise back with 'Corrections needed.'"

While Greg talked, Enid walked to her desk for her counterpoint book and notebook and flopped back onto her bed.

"Are you in bed?" Greg asked.

"No, it's OK," Enid said. "I was up. So there's like hard and fast rules for what you can do over barlines. You can land on thirds and sixths however you want, you're good there, but it sounds like you've got to do something different at that last part. You have to come at that perfect octave with contrary motion."

"Oh," Greg said. "Hard and fast. Got it." It sounded like he was writing. Enid could hear papers shuffling. "Ohhhhhh."

"No similar motion to a perfect consonance. So, you got it?"

"I'm getting it, Enid," Greg said. "Thank you so much."

"You're welcome," Enid said. She hoped Greg was the guitarist with the tooth gap. "Do you want to talk about the cambiata?"

"I'm good," Greg said. "What are you doing?"

"What? I'm—I was reading, and then you called."

"In bed?"

Enid laughed. "Well, yeah."

"Nice," Greg said. "Me too."

Enid relaxed into her pillow, kicked the counterpoint to the floor. It would be nice to have a friend in counterpoint.

Greg was quiet on the line for a few moments. Enid considered what questions she could ask that would help her place him without revealing that she didn't know who he was. But before she could think of anything, Greg spoke. "Counterpoint girl," he said, and now his voice sounded muffled and too close, like the receiver was pressed right up against his mouth. "What are you wearing?"

"Huh?" Enid said. She looked down at her T-shirt, a giveaway from a credit card company, and her sweats. "Like, just a shirt?"

"Just a shirt?" Greg huffed. "No pants, no panties?"

"Well, no, of course I have—" Enid started to say, but midsentence she realized what she should have realized before, when Greg asked what she was wearing. Or sooner, when he too quickly dropped the subject of the supposedly impossible counterpoint problem. Enid was momentarily horrified—she sucked in a big mouthful of air—but Greg heard her shocked gasp as something else.

"That's it," he said. "Touch yourself for me. Are you so wet?"

Enid meant to stand up and put the phone back on the receiver, but instead she slid one hand inside the waistband of her underwear and—her body didn't share in her outrage—she was in fact wet. "Oh," she said.

"That's it," Greg said. "I'm sucking your titties."

"Oh," Enid said. She assumed she was supposed to narrate something too, something she was doing to Greg, but she couldn't. She couldn't picture his face, much less any part of his body or what she'd be doing to it. So instead, she said, "That feels so good." She was shocked at the sound of her own voice—gravelly, breathy, sexy?—and that as she spoke, her fingers were even more slicked with wet.

Greg's breath was heavy now, his words came in self-contained bursts: "You're . . . wet . . . my . . . cock . . . s'hard . . . I'm inside . . . you . . . like that?"

Enid's traitorous hips rocked up off the flimsy dorm mattress. Her other unbusy hand floated up inside her T-shirt and clutched a breast, imagined it in the mouth of unfathomable Greg. "I'm so wet," she said, utterly unrecognizing of her body like this, and her voice, and her breath. Then they were both making sound at once and over one another, his low moans and *I'm fucking you so hard*, her *Oh*s and a *Yes, fuck me, Greg* here and there.

"I'm going to come, Enid," Greg said. "Oh god." He shuddered and moaned and as he did, Enid felt her insides go loose and she came, too.

And as soon as she did, as soon as it was over, she was returned to herself, and she was horrified all over again. Had she just had phone sex with a stranger? She felt disgusted, disgusting. It wasn't the sex part—she'd been naked with, come with, boys before; she could still thrill at the memory of that older boy, back home, peeling off first his own clothes, then hers on the freezing flat face of a rock beside the river, how the nearby falls misted their bare bodies and drowned out their sounds—it was the phone part. It was that she didn't know who was on the other end of the line, breathing now, and sort of moaning.

"That was nice," he said. And then, a long beat later, "Well, it's late."

"Wait," she said. "I want to see you."

Greg laughed. "You'll see me every Tuesday and Thursday. In counterpoint."

"No, I want to see you now," Enid said. This could be like a date—a date that maybe went too far, but that was still better than what she'd done here. If she could see him now, she could just mentally rearrange the order of events—first meet, *then* fool around, then . . . well, who knows? It was a seedy start, but maybe this was a redeemable romance.

"It's late," he said. "I have class early. And I don't even know where you live."

"I'll give you my address," she said.

"I think this was enough for tonight, Enid," Greg said. His voice was a normal volume now, but drowsy. Almost familiar.

"Please," she said.

He exhaled. Maybe he was smoking. "OK, fine. Address?"

A few minutes later she was on the grass, beneath the Chinese elm outside her locked dorm entrance, waiting for him. She'd changed her underwear, ashamed of her own smell, and armored herself in a bra. But Greg never showed. There were no messages on her answering machine when she finally went upstairs and there was no new, knowing intimacy with anyone in counterpoint. The Daves and Jasons and would-be Gregs moved around her, spoke over her, like always. And finally, after a few Tuesdays and Thursdays, just before Thanksgiving, she waited after class and asked Dr. Roderick if he knew when Greg was coming back to class. She had a book of his she'd like to return, she said, and then he looked at her for a long moment, smiling like he did, and said, "Greg? Who's Greg?"

Ever since then, there had been a tiny pebble of unease lodged in Enid's gut. She could ignore it when she was ensconced in her apartment or busy with class or practicing piano, or in daylight, when forty thousand people hurried about campus on skateboards or rollerblades. Now, as she passed with Gloria under that same Chinese elm outside her apartment, Enid half-considered telling her friend all of that. But there was too much to explain, not the least of which was phone sex itself. Gloria was a good sport, but she was a Victorian girl and Enid had read enough nineteenth-century novels to picture Gloria collapsing in a mortified swoon at the phrase "Fuck me, Greg."

Gloria stood still in the center of Enid's cinderblock apartment while Enid unburdened her arms and emptied most of the contents of her heavy backpack onto the desk: her music theory textbook with its rumpled sticky notes; scores (Gloria Clifford's chamber works and the Vieuxtemps sonata); the Vieuxtemps CD she'd checked out of the music library; *Ariel*, with her rough-draft essay stuck inside; her unfinished aleatory assignment and the fuzzy ibuprofen; the novel they were halfway through in Baggy Monsters. No wonder her back was killing her.

She left the two volumes of the music encyclopedia in the bottom of her backpack—safely out of sight—and kicked it under her desk.

"Do you live here all alone?" Gloria asked.

"Sure do. It's all mine," Enid joked, gesturing grandly at the dingy institutional carpet, the whitewashed brick, the chintzy furniture. "All four hundred square feet."

"But I suppose there's a house mother?"

"There's an RA. But she mainly just makes sure no one's keeping a kitten or smoking up."

"Don't tell me you smoke!" Gloria said, sounding scandalized.

When she turned back toward the center of the room, Gloria had arranged herself on the floor in front of the low bookshelf and was fixated, scandal forgotten, on the open volumes of the music encyclopedia that Enid had plowed through the night before. She was engrossed in Vol. 20, which Enid had left open, and after reading the Vieuxtemps entry ("It's quite sad," she sighed upon reading the entry's brief description of the stroke-induced end of Vieuxtemps's life), she flipped to the entry on Vivaldi. "This is some sort of compendium, then," she said, looking up from the floor over the tops of her wire-rimmed glasses and gesturing at the matched set of blue books on the floor around her.

"Yes," Enid said. "Like an encyclopedia? Of music. It was a gift from my mother."

"Wonderful," Gloria said in a hush, crossing her legs under her heavy skirt and reaching across with her long arms to scoop up a stack of volumes, which nestled into the bowl made by folds of fabric in her lap.

Enid stood with her back to her desk and faced Gloria, bracing for her inevitable questions. But Gloria was silent, drinking in the contents of the encyclopedias as if she were cramming for a test. Enid lowered herself to the floor beside Gloria and picked up a random book—Vol. 13: oh, hello, Modest Mussorgsky—mostly to have something to use as a cover as she watched Gloria. Every once in a while, her unruly brows would scrunch together or she would chew her bottom lip, as if puzzled by what she read, but she never said anything that would reveal to Enid what this visitor from 1910 was thinking as she glimpsed the future of music. If she was puzzled by the names she recognized that had been canonized, or those she sought but found had been forgotten, she said nothing. The two girls sat for a long while in silence, browsing, Enid losing herself in the past, in biographies of composers long dead before she was born, and Gloria, perhaps, in the future, sneak-peeking Gershwin and Ellington, Eno and McCartney.

After a while, Gloria pushed the books from her lap, stretched her legs out in front of her, and leaned back on her elbows. "I'm tired," she said. "I wonder what happens if I fall asleep here?"

"Didn't you sleep last night?" Enid asked. "Don't tell me you wandered the stacks of the library like a ghost."

"I don't fully remember," Gloria admitted. "Everything here feels like a dream to me. I might be dreaming now. I wonder what would happen if I closed my eyes?"

"I have no idea," Enid said. Gloria had posed her question musingly, but it made Enid sad. She had forgotten, briefly, that Gloria was just visiting. Their hours together that afternoon, with its duets and companionable silence, had been the first in a long time unmarked for Enid by a headache and bone-deep loneliness. She hated to think of Gloria's leaving again. "I wouldn't even know how to guess."

"Well," Gloria said, now lying back onto the floor and pulling her glasses off her face, "it could be a situation like Paul Prognosis and his crystal button, though I don't recall having any sort of accident."

"What? Who is Paul . . . Prognosis?"

"Oh, it's a book I read some time ago, when I was a girl. A fiction, certainly, but it does give one a few ideas. It did me, anyway."

"Accident? What happened to Paul Prognosis?"

"Fell. Hit his head something terrible and was unconscious for ten years! But then," here she snapped her elegant fingers in the air in front of her own face, as if she were both hypnotist and hypnotized, "he woke up right as rain on Christmas, with no knowledge of his illness, or the passage of time. Oh, it's a wonderful book!"

"It sounds really depressing," Enid said. Missing ten years of your life.

"Perhaps, but during that time he had simply the most thrilling adventures, Enid! He visited a dream city—Tone, it was called—and he learned all sorts of wonderful things and took in the most spectacular sights. And—this was my point—I think certainly he did sleep in Tone and awaken there, too, with no disruption to his great adventure."

Gloria chewed absent-mindedly on the end of her own braid, a habit Enid herself had been disabused of as a child. As thrilling as Enid found the exotic old-timey-ness of Gloria's phrasing and clothing, she found these shimmering moments of familiarity twice as thrilling.

"But then, there's also Ardath," Gloria went on.

"Your composer friend?"

"What? Oh no, dear, that's Adelheid." Gloria laughed. "Adelheid has no head for these things. *Ardath*."

"Who's Ardath?"

"Not a who, Enid. A *where*. Ardath is where the poet Theos goes to meet Edris, whom he met in a dream state, but then she disappears, so he goes to Al-Kyris, that's a dream city a bit like Tone, but not at all like this Arizona if you don't mind my saying so—which, that's where I keep getting hung up—they always go to beautiful utopias, not—I'm sorry, I shouldn't—"

"No, it's fine," Enid said. She'd never found her surroundings particularly Utopian, either. "So this is another book?"

"Oh yes, Marie Corelli. Have you read her?"

"No," Enid said. It had never occurred to her that women were writing wacko sci-fi a hundred years ago. It didn't sound like Enid's kind of book, but maybe it was. She could sense that she was becoming a different person than she'd been a long, strange day ago, before Gloria showed up. She made a mental note to look in the library stacks for Marie Corelli at the very least, or to ask her Baggy Monsters professor about her.

"Oh you must," Gloria said. "I'm just mad about her. Try *Thelma* first. Or *The Sorrows of Satan*. That is, if you're a reader of novels?"

"I am," Enid said. "In fact," and she stood and retrieved her half-finished Baggy Monsters novel from her desk, "I'm reading this now." She handed *Vanity Fair* to Gloria, who sat up to receive it.

"Thackeray! I've read this! I haven't nearly as much time to read since I've been at Pomeroy, and Langdon says I'll rot my brain—he reads strictly nonfiction, swears he never read a novel but under duress and he'll never read a novel again—but before I left home—oh, Daddy and I are both wild about Thackeray—"

Enid's mind snagged suddenly on a troubling detail about Langdon, brought on by this discussion of old literature, and setting it against what the encyclopedia had said about *Eepersip*'s inspiration. If Langdon had sworn off fiction, why did he eventually use *The House Without Windows*—not only a novel, but a novel by a *little girl*—as the basis for his great opera? It's not as if she could ask Gloria to help her figure it out. If the basic facts in the encyclopedia were right, the novel wouldn't be published for another seventeen years from Gloria's vantage point, and the opera would have to wait another eleven years after that. Gloria's disappearance, which Enid was beginning to suspect had something to do with the opera, was still thirty years in her future.

"Oh, and Dickens," Gloria was saying now, "although he scratches an altogether different itch for me. Have you heard of Mr. Dickens? I simply devoured *Bleak House*—"

"Of course," Enid said, and she entertained a flash of memory of performing in pancake makeup and burlap as unnamed Orphan No. 7

in a church production of *Oliver!* But before she could even begin to explain, Gloria continued chattering.

In Gloria's excited flurry of words, Enid picked out a few names she recognized—Thomas Hardy, George Elliot, Louisa May Alcott, authors she knew from childhood or AP English—but the rest were a jumble of almost-familiar but unremarkable names (Sarah Grand and Clara Louise Burnham and Robert Barr and Gertrude Atherton) and off-putting titles about captive princesses and penniless girls.

As she listened, Enid thought of the authors basking in the light of the *New York Times* Best Seller list even then and of her own favorites. Would *We Were the Mulvaneys,* which Enid had just read, be burnished, over a hundred years, to become *The Mill on the Floss,* or would Joyce Carol Oates's big novel oxidize into *American Wives and English Husbands*? Would Stephen King—he had been her Poppop's favorite—be to readers of the year 2100 a goofy relic, like whoever dreamed up that Paul Prognosis, or would he become Maine's own Jules Verne?

Gloria sighed and closed the book, her gaze fixed on the pile of blue books that spilled from the bookshelf, sitting in stacks and various states of openness. She scooted toward the wall and began lining the blue volumes up on the low shelf, taking care to place them in numerical/alphabetical order. When she was done arranging—and talking, for the moment—she announced to Enid, "You're missing two volumes. Number ten and . . . number . . . four." She looked up at Enid expectantly.

"Oh, yeah," Enid said. "Lost, I guess." She waited a beat, wondering if Gloria would realize that number four was where her own name would have appeared, but she didn't seem to. Of course not, Enid thought. It would take extraordinary hubris, or something, for a girl of twenty, given the chance, to look for her own name in the annals of history. Who would do such a thing?

"It's a shame," Gloria said, running a finger along the spines of the neatly arranged books. "I should have liked to see the entry on my Langdon." She stood and brushed the palms of her hands on her skirt.

"Your teacher," Enid said, leaning against the desk, under which her backpack emanated the heat of contraband.

"Oh, Enid, I wish you could meet him!" Gloria extended her long arms above her head, stretching her spine to the left and then the right. "He is brilliant." She looked around the small, unadorned space—the most interesting thing in it was the row of books they'd just perused—and settled into one of the chairs arranged by the small table.

"Are you sure you're not hungry?" Enid asked. The small digital clock beside her bed showed a few minutes past 9 p.m. "Do you want some tea or something? I have tea."

"I suppose a cup of tea would be fine," Gloria said.

"Aren't you worried about . . . ?" What was the polite way to say *pissing yourself*?

"They didn't cover that in *The Crystal Button*. I suppose I'm inclined to throw caution to the wind," Gloria said, laughing. "I'd like to have the full experience. An honest-to-goodness adventure."

"OK, then," Enid said, going into the small kitchen. She debated between the microwave and the small, two-burner range and a teakettle she'd brought from home. If it were just her alone, she'd nuke the water for tea, but having company (such special company!) seemed to call for more effort. She put two Sleepytime teabags in the mugs, filled her teakettle, and turned the burner on, and then returned to the doorframe. "How long have you been studying with him—with Langdon?"

"Two years now," Gloria said. A slight pink came into Gloria's cheeks as she spoke, cocking her head to the side and fiddling with the end of her long braid.

Of course, Enid thought. A teacher crush was hardly a modern invention.

When she'd entered Pomeroy in 1907, Gloria explained, it was as a violist. She hadn't even considered being a composer. It was Langdon who had put that idea in her head.

It happened at the beginning of the fall term a year later, at a reception for new faculty, of which Langdon was one. In fact, Langdon was the reason Gloria had attended the reception at all. Ordinarily she would have preferred to stay home, nose in a new book or practicing her instrument, but even those few weeks into the term Langdon, the new arrival, had caught her notice. "One can't miss him, you see—he's ever so much more, well, *fresh*-looking than the other teachers."

Enid thought of the picture in the book under her desk. That prim collar. That just-so hair. That mouth.

The reception to welcome Luther Langdon to the Pomeroy faculty had been held in September of 1908, at the start of Gloria's second year at the conservatory. It was a teatime affair, Gloria explained, held in a first-floor corridor at the school, lined for the occasion with wide, white wicker chairs. Between every third or fourth chair a small table had been set out with white linens and a sparkling silver tea service. Waiters circulated with trays of scones. The corridor seemed to Gloria an odd setting for an event, too narrow and feeling overall transient, a space between spaces more than a space itself. But she had to admit it was a grand non-space, lit by crystal chandeliers and wall sconces that shone off the polished marble floor, which was punctuated with rectangular, thick-pile Turkish rugs every few feet. The recessed doorways along the length of the corridor were paneled in polished dark wood that rose to support a blazing white and gently arching roof so high it was as if the planners had expected the gathering crowd to make use of scale, levitating, tea and scones in hand, to visit with one another.

As it was, though, the earth-bound students and faculty crowded the narrow corridor, which quickly grew stifling hot in Baltimore's September humidity, everyone eager to lay eyes on the famous new teacher. The faculty were excited by his résumé, the students by his photograph, which a resourceful gadabout named Adele had circulated in the days prior. Because Langdon was so tall, Gloria caught a fleeting glimpse of his handsome face down at the end of the corridor above the ordinary, less-fresh heads of the existing faculty, but she knew that unless she could levitate above the crowd and swim in the sticky, spacious air to the other end of the corridor, she had little hope of getting any closer to him. It's just as well, she thought to herself, contented with her glimpse of him and eager to return to her room, where a book awaited her.

She wanted to get out of the gown she'd worn. She could feel the delicate baby Irish lace of its yoke wilting in the damp heat. She felt suffocated under the broad-paneled linen dress, desperate to rip herself out of it, to send its twin rows of pearl buttons popping across the floor—*clickety tickety*—and kick her legs free of the heavy skirt finished in broad tucks at the hem, to loosen the apple-green suede belt that held her in, and, most of all, to pitch the insipid straw hat and its apple-green bow with mitered ends through the air like a skipping stone. She retreated from the reception corridor, aiming for the entry lobby with its grand spiral staircase. Before she got to the lobby, though, she found that one of the small offices off the hallway, usually locked tight when students were around, was standing open. Gloria stepped inside the cool, dark room lined with books. The sight (truly, it was more the smell) of a study made her intensely homesick just then, though her father had brought her back down to her aunt's house from Ohio for the new term only weeks before. He and Aunt Nettie had fussed over her, laid in pens and paper and books, new dresses and shoes and hats from Hutzler's, as if they were provisioning her for winter, which she supposed they were. Before he left, her father pressed into her hands a blue, cloth-covered volume, *The Beth Book* by Sarah Grand, and it was that delicious book, half-devoured, that awaited her now at home.

She was torn, then, between this space, which felt like her father's even though he'd never inhabited it, and her room in Aunt Nettie's mansion, appointed with all the beautiful things her father had bought her, things he'd actually touched and selected for her. Things, Gloria knew, which were not empty gestures in lieu of love but rather the material expression of an enormous love. Perhaps because it was just the two of them, her father had always been irrepressible in his expressions of love for her: it encompassed an expansive vocabulary not only of words, but of gestures, experiences, things. Gloria knew she was rich in every meaning of the term but she *felt* richest when she considered that she had never once questioned the deep, abiding love of her father.

(Upon hearing this, Enid felt an excruciating pang, remembering what Hockbein had told her about Gloria's drowned father. She knew what Gloria didn't: that his death was just three short years away.)

Gloria took a few steps toward the large desk and armchairs that anchored the room. She went to unfasten her hat only to find that she was still holding her napkin-wrapped scone from the reception. Looking back on this moment, she'd decided that the scene saved her some embarrassment. What if Langdon had found her there with her hat tossed aside, her hair unpinned and spilling wantonly over her sweat-sticky clavicle?

Instead, he found her seated at some trustee's desk, book open before her, and the scone between her teeth.

She had immediately engrossed herself in the story at the page she opened up to (Desdemona in a panic about her missing strawberry-embroidered handkerchief) and startled at the voice, sonorous and teasing, that resonated in the cool silence. "I hope you're not getting crumbs in the binding," it said, but not sternly.

She looked up to find Luther Langdon standing in the doorway in a gray frock coat and trousers, holding his gloves in his hand. He was twice as handsome as she'd feared.

"May I ask whose company you're finding more appealing than that of your classmates and esteemed faculty?" he asked, striding toward her. "Ah," he said as he circled and stood over the back of her chair, reading over her shoulder. "Now tell me, are you one of those bleeding hearts whose sympathies lie with poor, addled Othello? Or are you one of the conventional types who swoons for dashing Cassio?"

"Are those my only choices?" Gloria asked, having found her voice. "Because I rather think Iago steals the show."

"Iago!" Langdon laughed. He crossed behind her and stood facing her, just as Gloria stood to face him, the desk between them. "And may I ask what perverse beauty I have the pleasure of interviewing here?"

"I'm Gloria Clifford," Gloria said, astounded at his description of her. It wasn't *beauty* that threw her (among the many things her father had taught her was the incontrovertible fact of her beauty) but *perverse*. Not because she denied it—no, Gloria knew herself well and knew she could be mulish, obstinate, contrary, stubborn, willful, and intractable; in fact, she liked these untoward features of her personality because her father, perverse himself, liked them in her—but because Langdon had so quickly sized her up. She would think back on this exchange as their relationship bloomed, and what would stun Gloria was not the word itself but how very seen she had felt by Langdon in that moment of their meeting.

(Enid wanted to stop Gloria here: was she reading too much into a word? Couldn't this have been merely a throwaway line from Langdon, not evidence at all of his perceptiveness, but the kind of meaningless phrase that filled horoscopes? What other word would a person choose for a girl who expresses preference for the abject villain over tragic heroes and innocent casualties?)

"Well, Gloria Clifford, you're the very picture of a lady," Langdon said, taking in her lace and her linen, the precious rows of buttons, the apple-green suede around her waist. "One would hardly guess what perversity lurks behind such appearances. I'm Luther Langdon."

"I know," Gloria said. She came out from behind the desk and stood peering up at his handsome face.

"Of course," Langdon said, running a finger inside his immaculate collar. "It's quite warm here."

"I suppose it's different from England," Gloria agreed, the book still open in her palm. She looked down at it and saw that she had, in fact, gotten crumbs in the binding. Supposedly, Langdon had only disembarked from the SS Maryland a day earlier. The reception was so crowded because few had set eyes on the living man.

"Indeed. And you are a student here at Pomeroy. Cello?"

"I am a violist," Gloria said. "Second year."

"A violist," Langdon repeated, "with a head for literature."

"I suppose so," Gloria said. She snapped the book shut, hearing and feeling a faintly gritty friction in its spine.

"And do you limit yourself to a diet of such substance," he asked, glancing down at the book in her hands, "or do you sneak less edifying fare from time to time?" He used one of his fingers to brush a scone crumb from her lip.

It was shocking, really, that a man—an older man, a stranger to Gloria—would touch her in this intimate way. But her body was a beat or two behind her brain; heat bloomed happily across her cheek and her heart pounded in her chest. Her feet, which could have carried her a big step backward, or out of his reach entirely, remained planted on the floor, inches from his. If anything, her body tilted, of its own accord, ever so slightly toward him.

"I'm not sure I know what you mean," Gloria said, feeling sure now that Langdon had, by touching her mouth, pierced the protective tissue of etiquette that hung between them and that now he could see right through her, right into her skull and her chest cavity, each of which she imagined was lined with shelves stuffed full of the titles she'd read, not only *Ardath* and Paul Prognosis but also the novels of varying quality jammed in alongside adventure books for boys and *The Popular Science Monthly*. These shelves and their contents were a joint project of her and her father, who from the time Gloria was four years old had given her free run of his library, who told her to always "read against the grain." The finishing touches on the project—or its great renovation—were being provided by Aunt Nettie, herself with an enviably large library and an equally liberal policy regarding Gloria's access to it.

"Clifford. Your reputation precedes you. I'm told you're not a bad musician," Langdon said.

"You—you asked about me?" Why had he asked her who she was, Gloria wondered, if he already knew? It must have been a test. He was the professor, after all. She wondered if she'd passed.

"Imagine how I felt," Langdon said. "The man of the hour, fending off admirers left and right, then a fly in the ointment: one unruly creature who came only for the scones." He pouted like a dejected little boy, though Gloria could see close up that he was close to thirty-five. "I had to know who she was."

(Other things that are not modern inventions, Enid thought: hot guys who couldn't be happy unless every last girl wanted them.)

"So, yes. I'm told that you're a passable soloist."

"Passable?" Gloria asked.

"Don't tell me you fancy yourself a virtuoso?" Langdon said. He pressed his perfect lips together. "A girl like you?"

"What sort of girl am I?"

"The sort who fiddles her way sweetly from her father's house to her husband's without the sole of her fine shoe so much as touching the street."

"And what other sort of girl is there?" Gloria wanted to retract the stupid question as soon as she'd asked it.

"Go back to the reception and see for yourself," Langdon said. "That party is aswarm with smart girls in workaday eyelet. Your cohort Miss Hobart has probably got trousers on beneath her dress. She's going on about species counterpoint and eight-voice fugues with that awful voice of hers. She'll be onto the topic of the vote before long. I'm glad to miss it, to tell you the truth. It's sad to watch a party die, particularly by a lady's conversational homicide. Please don't take offense, dear. You're the preferable sort of girl."

Psyche was the smartest girl Gloria knew. She thrilled at the agility, the ferocity, of Psyche's mind. And Gloria loved Psyche's voice: low and rich. Psyche had read many of the books Gloria had read—they had torn through *Three Lives* together, over the course of afternoons and evenings taking turns reading to one another in the Forsyths' parlor—but where Gloria was a good reader, Psyche was, all in one indomitable form, simultaneously an enthusiastic devourer of stories *and* a real-life heroine *and* the sort of mastermind who could author them. Gloria was surprised to learn that Psyche was even at the reception; as of the day before, her plan had been to stay home and work on the suffrage essay she was submitting to a contest sponsored by the Just Government League. "The style should be virile," the column in *The Baltimore Sun* had said. "The more manly, the more the suffragists will like it." The girls had laughed at that and, when they got to the part that said, "real men like to be told of their weaknesses so as to correct them," they spent a good while speculating about what formative experiences or biological changes must take place in the male members of the species after boyhood, because none of the boys they'd known in school—Gloria in Ohio, Psyche in Indiana—had especially liked to be told of their weaknesses.

"The story on you, Gloria Clifford, is that that eccentric father of yours sent you to Pomeroy for a little finish and the chance to fiddle your way into some man's heart."

(Enid knew this move, too, from boys at parties who put their beery faces too close and said, "You think you're hot, huh? I don't see it," and that was supposed to make you want to make them see it.)

"And suppose I don't want a husband?" Gloria asked. (But she did!)

"Well, that would be a shame," Langdon said.

Gloria turned and slid the crumb-infested volume back into its empty space on the shelf—*find that handkerchief*, she thought, hopeless on doomed Desdemona's behalf—and rejoined Langdon in the center of the room.

"Why a shame?" she asked. Husbands seemed a great deal of trouble. Her own father had of course been a husband, once and rather briefly, but Gloria had never known him in that capacity. He still wore a ring, but only when it glinted did Gloria even remember that there had been a wife and, fleetingly, a mother.

"You don't strike me as the type to go around smashing conventions to bits like Miss Hobart. So why wouldn't you want a husband?"

"I don't know. Suppose I just don't? Suppose I'd like to be a virtuoso?" She jutted out her chin in the proud way girls in books did.

"How old are you?"

"I'm seventeen. Nearly eighteen. At Christmastime. What has that to do with anything?"

"Dear child," Langdon laughed. "Miss Clifford. It takes a certain kind of fortitude to be a virtuoso. Seriousness. It takes seriousness to be a tradition-smasher too, but of a sort of distorted type. Your foghorn friend Miss Hobart will probably do well in both regards, truthfully. She'll be wearing pants and penning operas throughout her perpetual spinsterhood. But you, you're a girl who skulks off at the first opportunity to find a nook for purloined cookies and storybooks." He touched her cheek. "It hardly smacks of any kind of seriousness, my dear. Shall we?"

Langdon offered Gloria his arm as if they were out for a promenade in the park. Stunned, she looped her arm into his and stepped out of the library, assuming he'd lead her back to the reception, fuming at his lecture but swooning at the thought of cutting a swath through that crowded room on Langdon's arm. Unbidden, the thought of the buttons on her dress flying off, *clickety tickety*, came to her and her cheeks steamed.

But he led her away from the reception, toward the lobby and the grand staircase. Was he seeing her out? Was he so affronted by her that he planned to usher her to the doors, deposit her on the street, and return to the party?

At the base of the staircase, Langdon paused to look at the marble statue. "I already quite love this fellow," he said, looking up at the dreamy-faced, strong-legged boy leaning against a post, idly fingering his flute.

Gloria was silent. Her heart pounded; she was desperate to forestall her expulsion but also to be free; she wanted to tell Psyche every detail of this confusing encounter, parse it with her. Of course, Psyche was back at the reception.

"I suppose he's become ordinary for you. I suppose all of this," he loosened himself from Gloria and took a step back, sweeping his arm across the marble lobby, the ornate ironwork staircase, the soaring ceilings, "is ordinary to a Forsyth."

No! Gloria wanted to scream, even as she nodded in answer to his question. None of this was ordinary to her. She loved this very spot intensely and anew every single day that she passed the sweet shepherd boy, every single time she heard the echoes of her feet on the marble stairs. But not because of its opulence—Langdon was right in one sense: her aunt's mansion made Pomeroy seem a grange—but because of the freedom it represented. Each day she flew away from the gilded cage of the Forsyth mansion and made her way two blocks east to Pomeroy, where she passed the shepherd boy and ascended the staircase on her way to the library, music lessons, lectures, concerts. The shepherd boy was her angel at the gates of a heavenly realm: where her mind roamed and skipped, where she ate her fill of Bach-bread and Schubert-honey, of rhetoric and composition. No, she had not become, by her dead mother's family wealth, inured to opulence as Langdon suggested. She'd just come to prefer opulence of the mind over the opulence of things. Brilliant Psyche could be counted on to point out, good-naturedly, that such a choice was one only made by people of means—that opulence of the mind depended on material opulence.

"I'm a Clifford," Gloria said. "Not a Forsyth. Technically."

(Enid shivered to think that she'd stood before that very same shepherd boy. Placed a patent-leather Mary Jane on those same marble steps.)

"Technically," Langdon repeated.

"Would you like to see more?" Gloria blurted then, louder than she intended to, her voice ricocheting around the marble lobby.

Langdon stepped back and peered at Gloria through his little glasses. "A personal tour?"

Gloria started up the staircase, and for a long moment she heard only a single set of footfalls, her own, on the steps. Soon, though, she heard a second set of steps—heavier—reverberating through the space. At first, Langdon's steps fit into the spaces between Gloria's, but by the time they reached the second floor, they were in perfect synchrony.

(Gloria paused just then, brow furrowed, mouth open, as if she'd forgotten something, or was trying to remember. Then she shook the forgotten whatever out of her head and went on with her story. *What? What is it?* Enid wanted to ask. *What do you remember? What is it about this staircase?* But the moment passed, and Gloria went on.)

"Come," she said to Langdon, whispering for no reason. She led him through a door at the top of the stairs and into an impressive wood-floored room with thirty-foot arched ceilings and a skylight. Late-afternoon sunlight streamed in, spotlighting the room from top to bottom. An elaborate plaster frieze ran the whole perimeter, a replica of the Parthenon frieze: horsemen and chariots, Olympians, girls. Below that, dark wood cabinets had been built into the walls, floor to ceiling, and inside each cubby of the cabinet sat a glowing bust: barechested and garland-draped heroes in immaculate marble and alabaster—Nero, Vitellius, Agrippa. The floor space was given over to pedestals of all heights, atop which stood white statuary of all sizes and position: gladiators in every state of combat and death, Minerva and Venus crouching, Polyhymnia and Venus standing, a boy and his goose, poor deserted Ariadne.

Langdon was silent as he followed Gloria through the room. They cut a weaving path beside a nymph at play, over to an athlete scraping sweat and dust from his muscled arms, behind Hermes holding baby Dionysus aloft, despite both of them missing some crucial limbs, and still Langdon said nothing. Gloria loved this space, but she rarely visited it. In fact, she'd last been here with Psyche, who'd shown the gallery to Gloria much in the way she was now showing it to Langdon, pointing out Venus de Milo and Silenus and Infant Bacchus, at which point Gloria had had to admit that her family had gifted the statues to Pomeroy; in fact, her family funded Pomeroy itself (an unseemly largesse Psyche graciously forgave).

Now, though, her silent tour with Langdon had led them to the corner of the room opposite where they'd entered, and Gloria stopped and found herself suddenly face to, well, *cock* (Enid's word, not Gloria's) with Hermes, nude but for a cap and a drape and a wand in his hand. She was second-guessing the wisdom of bringing Langdon here.

He was standing right behind her then, close, and Gloria could feel his heat, his breath on her neck, riffling the mitered ends of her hat ribbon. He put his big hands on her shoulders. With a different kind of man, this sort of excursion could spell disaster, Gloria knew, mostly from books. But she was here with Luther Langdon! He was famous, he was talented, she was safe.

(Enid wanted to interrupt to say, *It doesn't matter if you showed him Hermes's dick or the full tits of a wounded Amazon, you weren't asking for it.*)

After a long moment, Langdon said, "Well then. Shall we go back to the reception?" His voice had lost its sneering edge. He sounded tender to Gloria. "You go back down the way we came. I'll wait a beat or two."

"No," Gloria said. "You go back the way we came. There's another staircase over there, I'll go that way." She felt his hands leave her body, then his breath, then his heat. She heard his footsteps retreating.

"Wait," she said. "I—" Her voice echoed in the hard room. She turned away from Hermes and looked at Langdon in the doorway at the opposite side of the gallery.

"Yes?"

"I want you to know, Mr. Langdon. I am ... serious."

He laughed. "It seems so. I apologize. I was wrong about you." He bowed elegantly and left her there. She couldn't wait to tell Psyche that the *Sun* was right: real men liked to be shown that they were wrong.

By the time she finished her story, Gloria's tea had cooled, and she lifted her mug to her lips and pounded the whole thing, squinting afterward like it was Jägermeister.

"So . . . then what happened?" Enid asked.

"A few days later Langdon sent word that there was an open space in his composing studio. So I became his . . . student." Gloria peered into her empty mug. "I've learned so very much from him over these two years. He's wonderful."

"And did he ever, I mean, like, try to . . ." Enid was trying to find phrasing that wouldn't horrify Gloria. What was an old-timey way to say, *Did he ever pull any more creepy shit?* What was Victorian for *grabass*?

"No," Gloria said, straightening, her teacup reverie over. "I love him."

"Yeah, I kind of got that," Enid said.

"And he loves me. He's asked me to marry him."

That was a surprise. In the books Enid was reading for Baggy Monsters, men strode in to sitting rooms, sized up a girl by the looks of her needlepoint, and proposed marriage on the spot (oh to have the confidence of a tall, thick-haired heir to a baronetcy). Enid had figured this for literary hyperbole, but somewhere along the line—on the basis of one kind of weird near-hookup at a sculpture gallery and two years of composing lessons—Gloria's thirty-something teacher had decided his rich seventeen-year-old student would make an ideal twenty-year-old wife.

"I've been dying to tell someone," Gloria said, leaning toward Enid, eyes flashing.

"You didn't tell Psyche?"

"No," Gloria said. "I couldn't complicate things for her by asking her to safeguard a secret like that. He's her teacher as well, you know."

"It didn't sound like he was much impressed by her at first." Enid's phrasing sounded strange to her own ears: lacy, Gloria-inflected.

"I thought the same thing. But he invited her to the composing studio as well. Right after the reception, like he did me."

"And does she—does Psyche like him?" Enid had started to think of Psyche as a Victorian Ani DiFranco. It was hard to picture her worshiping a guy like Langdon. But whatever her problem was with him, she must have gotten over it. The encyclopedia said that Langdon launched Psyche's career.

"I suppose so." Gloria's thumb traced the bruise on her chin. "We haven't discussed him."

Enid had to revise the image that had formed in her mind, of two girls curled onto a chintz sofa, some novel tented on a chest that rose and fell with infatuated breaths, discussing every word that came from Langdon's devastating mouth. In two years of having the same hot teacher, they'd never discussed him?

"So are you going to do it? Marry him?" Enid couldn't imagine fielding marriage proposals from grown men. It was funny, really: a marriage proposal seemed to Enid an absurdly adult thing to contend with at twenty. But Gloria would probably feel the same way about Enid's mutual telephonic masturbation with a stranger.

"I want to. But I fear my father wouldn't approve."

"Why not?" Enid asked. "I mean, I probably wouldn't tell him about the sculpture gallery thing. But isn't Langdon like a big deal?"

"He is a 'big deal.' And I just know father would love him as much as I do—eventually."

"Why only eventually? Doesn't he want you to get married? I figured he'd expect it."

Gloria shrugged. "Of course he does. He wants me to be happy, and loved. But he always says, 'Don't marry the first man who recognizes your substantial gifts, dear. You can afford to be selective.'" It was funny hanging out with someone from a hundred years ago: just when you thought they were another species entirely, they said something totally relatable. Throw in a *honeybunch* and a noogie, and it sounded like something Enid's Poppop would've said.

"And does he? Langdon?"

"Does he what?"

"Recognize your, um, *substantial gifts*?"

"If you mean have we—?" Gloria prickled, indignant.

"God, no! But . . . does he think you're serious now? Like—" and then Enid tapped her temple and screwed up her mouth in what she hoped was the universal sign for "smart cookie."

"I should think so. He takes so much time with me. And I don't have the sort of trouble with him others do."

"Trouble? Who has trouble with Langdon?"

"Quite a few of the girls! Right after he joined the faculty, several asked to be switched to a different teacher. I think even Psyche has found him quite difficult."

"Oh?" Enid couldn't picture any pretty boy in a frock coat getting the better of good ol' Psyche.

"I'm sure I don't know. I haven't had any problems with him, and I've been his student for more than two years. But last spring, I happened to be going to the library to return a book when I saw Psyche going in for her lesson. And when I came down only thirty minutes later, she was leaving his office. In a state, too, I might add. He must have been quite critical. I've heard he can be that way." Gloria arched her eyebrows and flattened her lips in that way that said, *Not that I've ever seen it myself.*

"Did you talk to her?"

"No, poor thing, she was utterly discombobulated. Tears, the works. I've never seen Psyche cry. I didn't want her to feel abashed. She went into the washroom to put herself back together."

"Did you ever find out what happened?"

"No. I'm afraid Psyche and I haven't been spending much time together of late."

"What's that all about? I thought you two were BFFs."

Gloria scowled.

"You know, best friends. Forever. B-F-Fs."

"Oh, how adorable. I quite like that!" Gloria's smile faded as quickly as it had appeared. "We seem to have drifted apart over these last months. Of course, we're much busier these days, both of us. Our diploma concerts will be here soon. I do miss her, though. It seems I only see her coming and going from Langdon's office, and she's always in a hurry." Gloria shrugged. "That girl is involved in *everything*. I told you about the essay contest she entered?"

"You did."

"Not only entered—she won! I read about it in the *Sun*. The prize was twenty-five dollars—which I'm sure she put to good use—and a *trophy*. Money is a fine thing, but I think a trophy is just the jolliest thing, don't you?"

Enid's mind flashed to the drawerful of crappy mass-produced trophies she'd accumulated throughout childhood. She didn't have the heart to tell Gloria what intervening generations had done to the jolliness of trophies. "She didn't tell you herself?"

"She's always dashing off to some society meeting or another." Gloria rose from the table and wandered to Enid's dresser where she stood, back to Enid, uncapping lip balms and sniffing them.

None of this sounded quite right to Enid. How had they gone, in two years, from long afternoons in the parlor braiding one another's hair and devouring Gertrude Stein to being too busy to discuss a hot teacher or a writing victory? Somehow, Langdon loomed between the two girls, but Enid couldn't square it. She thought of the musical encyclopedias in her backpack, the incomplete clues they contained: Langdon married Gloria, but he had "launched" Psyche.

It was starting to seem that this "launch" was not a clean process of Langdon holding Psyche steady, building her, fueling her rockets, sending her off on her sparkling trajectory. Enid had learned in the third grade, on television, that a launch involved fire and shrapnel and danger. What kind of launch had Langdon given Psyche? And what role had Langdon played in the dissolution of the bond between these two friends? Was it professional jealousy or rivalry, or had there been another kind? There was no Encyclopedia of Girls' Friendships that Enid could consult. But oh if there were.

"What is this?" Gloria asked then, lifting the smoky-gray plastic cover of Enid's Aiwa stereo.

"Actually I was going to show you that." Enid moved from the table to her desk, reaching for the Vieuxtemps CD. "Here's that sonata you told me about. The one you played with . . . him." She brought the slim jewel case to the dresser and opened it. Gloria watched closely as Enid lifted a CD from the player, placed it into an empty jewel case, and replaced it with the Vieuxtemps disc. As Enid powered up the stereo, she handed the jewel case to Gloria, who inspected the cover. "Who is Bruno Giuranna?" She pointed to the gray-haired man bowing a viola on the cover of the disc.

Enid shrugged. "It's the only recording of the Vieuxtemps the library had."

Gloria watched closely as Enid closed the CD changer lid, powered on the stereo, and pressed play. Immediately, the opening bars of the first movement of the Vieuxtemps viola sonata filled the room: the viola's throaty opening in B-flat, drowsy descension to D, the languorous ascension to its home note. The piano's arcing rainbows of fully voiced chords over four octaves of keys.

Enid thought, not for the first time, how astounding it was that you could learn music as a child in the twentieth century—a year or two of piano lessons was all it took—and you were able to speak and understand the musics of hundreds of years. Other languages didn't work that way. You couldn't learn to speak English in the 1980s and expect to make perfect sense of documents from 1600, expect to be able to converse with an English speaker from 1791 with total ease. Only music worked that way, and its sibling, math.

Just as Bruno Giuranna shifted into the flashy allegro section of the first movement, Enid said, "Oh wait, you're really into the second movement, right? We can skip to that." Enid reached one finger toward the skip track button, but Gloria grabbed her wrist.

Gloria turned her astounded gaze to Enid. Her mouth hung open and her eyes flashed between Enid's and the small speakers that flanked the stereo. "All of that sound is coming from *there*?"

"Great, right? So do you want to hear the second movement?" Enid thought of Gloria's twilight visits to Langdon's office, their clumsy duets.

"No, I don't think so," Gloria said, turning to face Enid. "I hope you won't mind my saying this. It sounds too . . . perfect."

Enid, weaned on LPs, had to agree. CDs were miracles—she had towers of them throughout the apartment, and stuck in fat black CD wallets, purchased at the local buy-sell-trade record store on a credit card at a shockingly irresponsible rate—but she longed for the pop and hiss of lo-fidelity recording, for the sneeze and crackle of live music. CDs pressed all of that into a dense sonic laminate. Shiny, hard.

"Tell me," Gloria said, suddenly looking stricken—homesick—and sad. "What would you be doing tonight if I weren't here?"

Enid laughed. "Not really anything different." The unfinished aleatory assignment clamored at her.

"Do you expect any callers?"

The careful trans-century translation efforts went both ways, but Gloria's pity was clear.

"No, I don't have a boyfriend, if that's what you mean." Back home, she'd had her share of action. Even here at school, her time had been punctuated by a series of "relationships" with townies and wannabe poets that followed, basically, a three-movement form of their own: coffee date, hookup, breakup. Lately, though, there'd been no one. Just disembodied Greg, and the brown-eyed boy who worked at the record store, for whom Enid carried a torch, hence the reckless spending.

Gloria shrugged. "But have you any friends?"

"No," Enid said. That was the short answer.

The long answer—which she hoarded, guiltily, even though Gloria had spilled her guts about Psyche and Langdon and spinster Aunt Nettie, and dear old dad, and all her favorite books—was also no, but no-with-an-asterisk. Enid had *had* friends. In high school, she ran with a passel of cold, cruel girls she stayed with because it was safer to be among them than to be someone they laughed at. In her first year at this big dumb college, she'd fallen in briefly with a thrilling and reckless art student from Pittsburgh who tried her level best to be thrilling and reckless at a perpetually sunny, football-crazy state school but ultimately had to transfer to a real art school in a real city to reach her full thrilling and reckless potential.

In the music school, there were a handful of girls she ached to befriend: a wise-cracking violist from England; a saxophonist she'd once overheard telling a charming story of a neighbor's pet buffalo back home in Missouri; a flautist with a gazillion brothers and sisters and a beloved clunky old car that ran on diesel. Much to Enid's frustration, the universal language of music wasn't much help. Even in music school, relationships were hammered out in many mystifying argots: *You doing anything Friday? Hey, I think you're in my theory class? You tryna get a bagel after this? You smoke up? On your way to the dining hall? I'll walk with you.* For all she knew, *Hey, what pitch is this?* was an overture. Enid never got any better at this language, no matter how much she practiced. It was a shame, she thought, to trade in ordinary language at a music school; it was as if they all knew Esperanto but refused to use it.

"Not really," Enid said again, in response to Gloria's bruising question.

"Well, I don't want to be in your way," Gloria said. "Please carry on as though I'm not even here."

"Then I think I'll take a shower, if it's all the same to you."

"Please," Gloria nodded, still holding the Vieuxtemps jewel case. "I'll be here."

Until she said that, Enid hadn't realized how much she hoped it was true, or how flimsy an assurance it was. How could Gloria know that whatever mechanism brought her here wouldn't suddenly whisk her back—to 1910, to Langdon? To that grand staircase where, Enid was beginning to suspect, something awful had happened to Gloria? Paul Prognosis had fallen and hit his head; maybe Gloria had, too, even if she didn't remember it. And maybe she hadn't simply fallen.

As she stepped out of the shower and reached for her towel, though, she was reassured. From the other side of the thin wall came music she recognized and the distinctive clatter of plastic jewel cases being stacked and sorted. Gloria, quick study, had figured out the shuffle function and was putting it to manic use.

As Enid re-entered the room, she was greeted by ear-splitting Icelandic electronica.

"You're going to have to turn that down, or Stormy will be over here in no time to write me up," Enid laughed, towel-drying her hair with one hand and adjusting the volume with the other.

"Stormy?" Gloria asked. The music had worked on her like wine coolers: she was pink, easy, glittering. "What sort of a name is *Stormy*?"

"You're one to talk," Enid said. "Ebbe? Adelheid? *Psyche*?"

"Those are hardly unusual names where I come from," Gloria laughed, sparring now. "If anything, *Gloria* is the oddity. I've always felt my name was out of place, anyway."

"Same," Enid said. "So how did you end up a Gloria, if it's such an unusual name?"

"My father said that he heard church music when he first laid eyes on me. But he wasn't very devout, so he grabbed the first sacred musical phrase he could recall to name me. He could only remember—and spell—the Gloria part. I'm lucky my name isn't Gloria In Excelsis Clifford."

"Your father named you? Didn't your mother get a vote?"

"She passed in childbirth," Gloria said. "It's always been just me and father. Oh, how I used to hate being called Gloria. But I rather like my name now."

"What's the secret?" Enid asked. She hadn't completely outgrown wanting to be a Heather, an Amanda. Yet another Jennifer.

"When I was twelve, I read a book—you recall I told you about Marie Corelli?"

"The sci-fi chick?"

"It was one of hers—this one is called *Temporal Power*, and in it there is a whole character called Gloria. Found as a baby..."

"I guess I just need a dreamy romance starring an... Enid," Enid snorted. "I won't hold my breath."

"So you haven't read *Idylls of the King*, then?"

"No," Enid said. *Add it to the list*, she thought. "Are you a Björk fan now?"

"Oh, I should say not. But this—" Gloria pawed through the discs, which she'd clearly sorted into piles according to preference. She reached for a CD by Enid's all-time favorite artist, a classically trained, flame-haired singer-songwriter who had her way with her enormous Bösendorffer like it was a Stratocaster. "This!"

Enid got chills. The singer-songwriter was her favorite not only for the way she layered erogenous moaning over thrumming harpsichord, not only for her poetic lyrics, but also because she was from the same town in Maryland Enid was from. Had even attended her own high school. Enid felt proprietary toward her, felt the same claim she imagined believers felt for their patron saints. And like a saint—a grinding, dirty-mouthed, absurdly talented saint—this singer-songwriter was the stuff of legend. As a high-schooler, she'd moonlighted at piano bars at the beach. As a child, she'd been the youngest pupil admitted to none other than Pomeroy.

"Excellent choice," Enid said. "I've got more of her if you want."

"I have had enough music for now. Do you ever feel that way? As if the music-receiving part of your brain is a sponge, and sometimes needs to be wrung out before you can listen to another note?"

"I do." For Enid, an over-musicked state felt like the moments after an orgasm, when the slightest touch could send her into a shudder, aftershocks of pain following pleasure. But the sponge metaphor was better for "mixed company," as her Poppop might've put it.

As glad as she was to have Gloria's company, Enid was starting to feel the same anxiety she'd always felt as a child at sleepovers. When you'd had pizza and made popcorn and watched a movie and... it was 10 p.m. and you had to figure out what to do with the next twelve hours with a near-stranger. "Do you want to, um, read?"

"That's a terrific idea," Gloria said. "Aren't you midway through *Vanity Fair*?"

"Yeah, and actually I do need to get caught up on it for class."

"Let's read that!" Gloria skipped over to Enid's desk and grabbed the book, flipped to Enid's bookmark, and settled herself on the floor, her back against the bed. Enid sat on her bed as Gloria began to read aloud.

When Enid made the suggestion, she had pictured more of a parallel play situation: each with their own book, quiet (the state she engineered those childhood sleepovers to, until the invitations stopped coming).

Apart from a few gravely intoned readings in her confessional poetry class, Enid hadn't been read to—really read to—since childhood. But a few sentences into the chapter, Gloria had the prose aloft like a kite, and Enid recalled how in elementary school the children sat on a mustard-colored rug to be read to, and though she and her classmates would start out in an orderly circle, all sitting cross-legged and alert, if the story was good and the teacher was kind, they could melt into various shapes of blissed-out repose, heads on one another's laps, or braiding hair or running tiny fingers up and down spines, a tender thrill they called "doing racecars." When she got to junior high, the teachers stopped reading to the children and the school had a whole rule about kids never ever *ever* touching one another, even for high-fives. Enid had forgotten about those serene mornings on the mustard rug, and now, as Gloria sat reading to her, close enough to touch, the sensation of being petted, plaited, and stroked came back to her and she curled into her pillow, contented in a way she'd forgotten how to be.

She was nearly asleep—but, somehow, alert to the story—when

Gloria reached the end of the chapter. "Now your turn," she said, passing the book up to Enid.

Enid backed up against the cinderblock wall and read. She got so absorbed in the story that she forgot that she was doing homework. She forgot, in fact, about the unbelievable circumstances that had brought into her dorm room a long-vanished, presumably dead woman—no, the girl that woman had been *before* she became a woman, or vanished, or dead—a girl who had now curled herself into a ball at the foot of her bed, resting her cheek on one of Enid's folded sweatshirts.

Enid let the book rest across her chest and watched Gloria sleep. She had taken off her wire-rimmed glasses and held them in her hands under her chin, as if they were a clutch of buttercups. Her chest rose and fell, adagio, under that pintucked blouse.

Enid wondered what Gloria was dreaming of, what was behind the furrow in her brow and the slight smile on her lips. Was dreaming even possible? If Gloria's visit to Enid was only a kind of dream, a lucid dream, then it didn't seem possible to Enid that Gloria could double-dream, could dream within the dream.

Enid was certain that *she* was awake, though, that all this was really happening. Even spending time with Gloria—apart from the transcendent sonata they'd played together—hadn't felt dreamlike in the falling, flying, talking-animals-and-melting-clocks sort of way. Talking and playing music and reading and walking and being silent and having tea with Gloria felt natural and intimate and easy, which, Enid realized, was the elusive kind of friendship she had always longed for.

Enid felt protective of Gloria as she watched her sleep. She looked vulnerable and very young. She was disturbed by much of what Gloria had shared. She may not have had a lot of direct personal experience with having a best friend, but Enid had been doing, since the first grade, a deep ethnography of the best-friendships around her: Elisa and Julie, Lauren and Jenny, Ellen and Sherry, Molly and Sylvia, Beth and Sarah. And, at one point, there had been Gloria and Psyche, but now something strange was going on. The fraught distance between the girls had something to do with Luther Langdon.

That was what really bothered Enid. Something was *off* with this dashing older man who had arrived in Baltimore in 1908, promptly sweeping a seventeen-year-old Gloria off her feet and making her his student. Within two years' time, he would decide to marry her. Enid just couldn't imagine it. What if she went into Dr. Roderick's office hours, as she sometimes did for help on counterpoint, and he just up and proposed to her? Dr. Roderick was probably thirty-five to Enid's nineteen, so about the same age difference, and there was no question he was handsome like Langdon, she even thrilled sometimes when she found herself trading pleasantries in an elevator with him, yet she couldn't fathom *a thing* existing between them as had happened between Gloria and Langdon.

And what happened at the top of that grand staircase?

Enid had been so sleepy while Gloria was reading, but now she couldn't quiet her brain. She didn't think she would be able to sleep, and anyway, she still hadn't finished her aleatory assignment. She draped a blanket over Gloria and went to her desk. She put *Vanity Fair* back into the backpack with the two blue books—she couldn't put those back on the shelf now, where Gloria could spot them—and pulled out her assignment.

Working only by the light of her feeble desk lamp, she set out to finish the stupid aleatory assignment. Nothing about the exercise felt like composing to her, or like music, though it was vaguely satisfying in a stoichiometric way. Enid waited for the profound boredom she felt to turn into something else—John Cage himself had been a proponent of boredom. "The way to get ideas is to do something boring," Hockbein had quoted his idol as saying. "They fly into your head like birds." Of course, Hockbein didn't think his Cage-y assignment would be boring to anyone in the class; he was suggesting that the young composers do something boring like hiking to increase the chances they'd be bird-bombed by ideas.

No birds came, but morning did, and Enid's assignment was as good as it would get, and Gloria lay there still, in a stripe of sunshine slatting through the chintzy blinds, a trail of drool across her cheek.

Enid dressed as quietly as she could, but as she bent over to tie her Docs, Gloria asked, in a tiny, raspy voice, "Did I sleep? Am I here?"

"You did," Enid said. "And you are." She had stolen glances, all through the night as she worked, to make sure that Gloria was still there, her faint snoring a breathy descant over Enid's thrumming fingers on her desktop, figuring rhythms as she worked, and whispering to herself fragments of text. *In the freakish Atlantic / where it pours bean green over blue.*

"And you?" Gloria asked, standing, yawning, and folding the blanket.

"I'm here."

"Did you sleep?" She thumbed crust from her eyelids.

"Afraid not. Had to finish this." She brandished the assignment just before filing it into her backpack with the two books she'd kept from Gloria. Gloria wrinkled her nose at the sight of Enid's "composition."

"It looks like you're ready to go," Gloria said.

"Just about," Enid said, stuffing her backpack. "You're welcome to stay here while I'm gone. I can come back later on to check on you." But then Gloria shifted uncomfortably, and Enid realized that her friend didn't want to be here alone, caged all day. "Or you're welcome to come to class with me."

"Do you mind if I freshen up first?" she asked. Her clothes were rumpled.

"Sure," Enid said. "And help yourself to something clean to wear, if you want." She gestured at the meager closet, its thin accordion door bunched to one side.

"Oh," Gloria said. "I . . ."

"Not your look?" Enid laughed.

"Forgive me for saying so," Gloria said, taking in Enid's boots, her striped T-shirt, her gaping overalls and the hoodie she was just now pulling on. "Everyone here dresses like a farmer or an urchin."

Enid laughed again and went to the closet. She directed Gloria to the section in the back where she kept her recital clothes: black trousers; a black floor-length skirt; a black, calf-length velvet dress with a modest scoop neck and long sleeves; an assortment of plain white blouses. Concert dress. "Knock yourself out."

As they crossed campus together that morning in their nearly matching boots—Enid's Doc Martens peeking from under the frayed cuffs of her overalls, Gloria's heeled calfskin button boots under the folds of Enid's flowing concert dress—Enid felt deliriously overtired but intensely happy. Finally—finally!—she was one half of one of those friend duos she'd seen so many times walking to class. Was it premature to claim Gloria as her best friend after less than forty-eight hours? Premature, and also immature? Probably. And did it matter that Gloria was invisible to everyone but Enid? Enid thought no. What mattered to her was that she had someone to share clothes with, someone to walk with, silent or swapping meaningfully arched eyebrows and telepathic half-sentences.

When they passed in front of the student union, they found themselves swallowed up by a small crowd assembled in front of a bus parked on the walkway. "Choose or Lose" was painted across the front and sides of the bus, in meticulously lettered faux-graffiti. A long-haired, bare-footed boy in corduroys and a flannel shirt with rolled sleeves jutted his chin at Enid, smiled, and tossed his curls off his shoulders. "Hey, you," he said. "What's your major?"

"What? Me? Music, I guess."

"So rad," he said. The boy was making such unbroken eye contact, it was rattling. "We love music," he said, gesturing behind him at the bus, on top of which Enid now saw was a big cube with the MTV logo on all sides, a blown-up version of the one that collared the microphones of network VJs. "I mean, obviously. What's your name?" He put one suntanned arm around her and pulled her away from the crowd, toward the bus.

"Enid."

"OK, Enid the Music Major, you don't seem apathetic to me."

"Who said I was?" Enid looked back, but she'd somehow lost sight of Gloria in the crowd.

"Well, not you individually, but voters like us—I'm guessing you're between eighteen and twenty-four, right, Enid?—they think we don't care. About jobs, or clean water, or anything."

Enid prickled. Apart from the most abstract, unexamined position that jobs were good, and clean water was good, she didn't really have thoughts on the issues of the day. She was registered to vote and expected to cast a ballot for Bill Clinton in a few weeks, but beyond that, she hadn't thought about it. She searched the crowd for Gloria. In her long black dress, with her pale skin and long hair, she should have stood out, but Enid couldn't find her.

"... so we're traveling across the country, hooking up with young people like you—like us—to make sure they get out there and vote. Cool?" He held up the stack of empty voter registration forms in his hands. "Choose or lose, you know."

"Yeah, cool," Enid said. Taking her "cool" as an indication that he'd found his next mark, the boy tugged her away again, to a long table set up beside the bus.

"Woah, OK. You ready to lose your voter virginity?" the boy said, handing Enid a pen.

"Oh, wait, sorry. I'm already—"

The boy moved closer, put a hand on her shoulder. "Enid. Don't bail on me now. Voting is a big responsibility. I get why you might be freaked. It's like when I got my driver's license, I was like, 'Woooooah, I could totally annihilate someone with my mom's Ford Taurus,' right?"

Enid nodded.

"Voting is totally like that. Totally. But, getting my driver's license also meant I could leave campus for lunch. Like, I could get Taco Bell whenever I wanted. I had *choices*, dude. Voting is totally like that, too, Enid." His tone shifted then, from rip-off Pauly Shore to statesman:

"And unlike a driver's license, voting is your *right*. So just fill that out, and give it to us, and boom, you're registered. Election Day is November fifth, OK?"

"Isn't it too late? The election is only—" Enid scanned the minirally, speakers pulsing with 311 singing "Down" even in the too-early morning and boys in MTV "Rock the Vote" T-shirts brandishing T-shirt guns, looking for her way out, looking for Gloria.

"No way, dude," the boy beamed. "In this state, you can register right up to Election Day." He showed her the back side of the ID badge that hung around his neck, with a laminated list of all the states and their registration deadlines in tiny print. "See?"

"I'm sorry." Enid stepped back and moved free of the boy's arm; as cute as he was, she wanted to get away.

The boy's smile fell and his eyes flamed. He grabbed Enid's upper arm. "This matters, OK? This, like, fucking *matters*."

Enid turned to the form. There were so many boxes. But only the ones shaded in red were required, so she whizzed through those, pausing only slightly at the last, which required her to certify, with a signature, that the information she'd provided was true.

"OK, here you go." She pushed the completed form and pen across the table. "Sorry, I have to get to class." She pushed past the boy and into the crowd.

"Sweet," the boy called after her. "Don't forget. November fifth. Rock the vote."

"Right, rock the vote," Enid said. She cut between two people playing hacky sack and, finally, there she was. "Let's go," she said, relieved.

When they were clear of the crowd, Enid finally exhaled. She stopped and turned to Gloria. "I was afraid I'd lost you. I didn't see you for a second. Also, congratulations, I guess," she said.

"Whatever for?" Gloria asked.

Enid thought of Gloria's friend Psyche, penning her contest-winning essay while her goal, her suffragist triumph, was still ten years in the future.

"I just registered you to vote."

They were late to Dr. Doyle's class. He had already issued whatever weird greeting he had for the class that Friday morning, and he was standing at the edge of the stage rubbing at a stain on his white shirt. "We'll start with some listening today." Late as they were, Enid and Gloria took the first seats they spotted.

Enid expected Dr. Doyle to produce a record and make his way to the turntable on stage, but instead he walked over to the grand piano and pulled back its quilted cover. "Go ahead and get out your notebooks," he said as he opened the fallboard. He hooked one foot around the leg of the bench and pulled it out. "We'll do it a little different today—no recording. Live performance."

Enid scanned the edges of the stage, hoping a secret guest star would trot out. Instead, Dr. Doyle settled himself on the padded bench and swept the rumpled tails of his sport coat out from under him. "You know what to do. Write down everything you hear."

There was a brief wave of noise as backpacks were unzipped, notebooks folded back on their squealing spiral bindings, pens uncapped in teeth. A few murmurings: of course theory and composition professors had to be accomplished musicians, but had anyone ever seen them *play* anything? "Ready?" Dr. Doyle said, rubbing his palms along the tops of his thighs.

When the room had quieted sufficiently, he raised his hands theatrically and positioned them over the keys. And then—nothing.

There were a few titters—old Dr. Doyle choked! Stage fright, really? What a hack—but when he continued to sit there, hands over the keys, eyes shut and swaying slightly, the whispers took a different tone: was he having a stroke?

It was Gloria who caught on first and started whispering to Enid. She pointed to Enid's paper, as if instructing her to take dictation. "Nasal congestion—mild, toward the front row," she said, and Enid wrote it. "Water in pipes—lavatory?—rushing."

After what felt like an eternity but couldn't have been more than a minute, Enid heard a piano. She opened her eyes to see if it was Dr. Doyle but he only sat there, frozen before the keyboard, his hands folded in his lap. Still, the piano continued, a frantic dance of staccato eighth notes in 6/8, a pattycake of dense triads—F-sharp major trading off with a minor—then a glissando screaming up the keyboard and descending in two octaves of chromatic runs. Enid looked to her right. Gloria's eyes were open, and she looked around wildly, as if she heard it too.

On the half-size folding desk in front of her, Enid's notebook lay open. She'd written only what Gloria had dictated, and even though she heard music now, she wrote nothing more. She let her pen fall to the floor, where it clattered. No doubt, her classmates recorded the clattering. But not Enid; she put her hands out in front of her on the notebook, positioned them over a phantom piano and began to play. The notes she was hearing transmitted directly to her fingers, and her fingers tapped out this novel music. Perfectly. Sight-reading in the truest sense of the word.

When she shut her eyes again, she could see it as well as hear it. The score scrolled across her eyelids, the piano part and the viola part above it. A measure of 9/8. Four of 6/8. A measure of 9/8. *Meno mosso. Leggiero. Sempre piano*. Two pages of full-fisted arpeggios while the viola sang. To her right, she could feel Gloria next to her. Not body heat, exactly. Electricity. Gloria next to her made the hairs on her arms stand, and they waved in the still air of the classroom. It was as if Enid had transformed into an instrument herself—a theremin, maybe—and she heard (when she finally shared this story, decades later, she would *swear* that she heard) the throaty voice of the viola line cutting through the room, coming from charged space between their arms, coming from Gloria.

For the next three-plus minutes, eyes closed, Enid heard and played the second movement of a sonata for viola and piano that didn't yet exist. She and Gloria played together, their silent and invisible duet filling the concert hall, mordents and trills added by the traffic noise on the street outside, the human sounds made by her classmates, her own blood pulsing in her temple.

The four-and-a-half minutes of supposed silence in that recital hall, framed as it was by Dr. Doyle seated at the piano as if he were performing, transformed noise into music. Scraps of sound and thought became information, became meaningful. Enid felt, finally, like a composer. She glimpsed, briefly, a fully formed whole, a tree on a hill backlit by lightning, illuminated perfectly for a fleeting instant, an image that would sustain her through years of decidedly slow, laborious, dark work, years of pen scratching paper to render any part of the hot urgency of all in that moment she saw, and heard, and knew:

That the sonata coursing through her body hadn't yet been written but would be, in 1919, by the composer seated to her right. That Gloria would go home to Pomeroy having glimpsed, here in 1996 with Enid, the piece that would make her a real composer: the viola sonata. Before she could compose it, though, she'd have to leave this place and return home, to resume her life in 1910, where she would wake from a tumble down the stairs to find her teacher-turned-suitor awaiting her with his cold eyes and lusty mouth.

And she knew, too, that the voice that had said, "Very nice again, Enid" as he slid her counterpoint homework across the desk—she realized it now, or she recognized it—was in fact the same voice that had said, "I'm sucking your titties" on the phone that night last fall, the same voice that had thrummed with secret amusement when she'd asked after her mysterious classmate: "Greg? Who's Greg?" That Dr. Roderick was the rightful owner of that pebble of unease, but he'd made it hers to hold.

She knew then that she would not turn in her aleatory assignment. That she would withdraw from her music classes on Monday and flee to the English department, where she would not risk running into Dr. Roderick. That she could set aside, for now, her feelings about failing as a musician and find relief in the bracing urgency of self-protection.

That she would not be a composer, after all. At least, not of music.

That she would spend the weekend alone in her brick apartment prolonging her time with Gloria after she'd gone by reading the books that had made her: *Vanity Fair* and some Dickens, *The Beth Book* and Paul Prognosis and the wild Marie Corelli novels, if she could find them at the library. That she'd listen to the opera *Eepersip* at top volume on her Aiwa stereo while reading *The House Without Windows,* and this exercise would finally allow her to reconcile the serious Luther Langdon, who'd sworn off fiction, with the opera's source text: an enchanting novel by a little girl.

That Gloria's bruises would heal and she would forget having argued with Langdon at the top of that marble staircase—the same staircase she'd climbed ahead of her handsome teacher, heart pounding, on the day they met, two years earlier. She would forget what she said, and what he said, two years later on the very same staircase, just before she went plummeting to the lobby, crumpled and concussed at the feet of the marble boy with his silent flute.

That after her beloved father drowned in Dayton, Ohio, Gloria would marry Luther Langdon, a philanderer and perhaps worse, who would devote his energies not to launching her career but his own and, motivated by shame or guilt, that of her onetime best friend, Psyche.

That he would devour her family funds and drain her substantial gifts and turn Gloria from a genius to a sad wife. That her marriage to Langdon would be among the griefs that caused her to stop composing for many years, living in a housecoat in an upstairs bedroom subsisting on novels, and that when she finally found her way back to the page (a triumph!) he would premiere her great opera *Eepersip* under his own name.

That Langdon's theft would ruin Gloria the composer, but not Gloria the person. That, just as a whole piece of paper is rendered scrap when a child cuts a perfect circle from its center, Gloria could respond to Luther's ultimate violation by absenting herself entirely. That, somehow, Gloria—the remnants of her, the intact edges of herself she still recognized as herself—would leave Langdon. That, with help from someone or several someones, Gloria would not disappear; she would *depart*. That there is a difference.

And that she, Enid Bluff, music-school flame-out, would be the sole possessor of this fuller and truer account, the only person capable of correcting the meager encyclopedia entry of the great American composer Gloria Clifford.

Enid knew that when she opened her eyes, Gloria would be
—and she was—
gone.

ACKNOWLEDGMENTS

I want to thank Kelcey Ervick for selecting this story and for her keen and generous editorial guidance. I am grateful to everyone at Miami University Press: Jody Bates for his expert editorial eye, good humor, and unflagging patience; Allison Huffman for her nuanced copyediting; Jeff Clark for the beautiful design; Keith Tuma for his tireless work in shepherding the press; and Amy Toland for her stewardship of my work from manuscript to book. Thank you to my mom and my husband, Fred, for their endless confidence in me, and to my very real friends with infinite patience for my babbling about my imaginary friends: Courtney Rath, Marc Oxborrow, and Michelle Hill. My music school friends were close to my heart for this story—most of all the saxophonist, composer, and educator Beth Schenck, whose album *Above and Below* was on frequent rotation as I wrote. Finally, I am grateful in advance for my readers.

ABOUT THE AUTHOR

Andrea Avery is the author of *Sonata: A Memoir of Pain and the Piano* (Pegasus Books), which is being adapted for the stage. Her work has appeared in *Barrelhouse*, *CRAFT Literary*, *Ploughshares*, *Oxford American*, *Real Simple*, and other places. She holds a B.A. in music, an MFA in Creative Writing, and an Ed.D, all from Arizona State University. She is working on a novel.